840L

DATE DUE

DEMCO, INC. 38-2931

GAYLE BRANDEIS

MY LIFE WITH THE LINCOLNS

HENRY HOLT AND COMPANY

NEW YORK

Henry Holt and Company, LLC
Publishers since 1866
175 Fifth Avenue
New York, New York 10010
www.HenryHoltKids.com

Library of Congress Cataloging-in-Publication Data
Brandeis, Gayle.
My life with the Lincolns / Gayle Brandeis.—1st ed.
p.   cm.
Summary: In 1966 Illinois, twelve-year-old Wilhelmina, convinced that she,
her parents, and sisters are Abraham Lincoln's family reincarnated, determines
to keep them from suffering the same fates, which is complicated when she and
her father become involved in the Civil Rights Movement.
ISBN 978-0-8050-9013-0
[1. Family life—Illinois—Fiction.   2. Civil rights movements—Fiction.
3. Lincoln, Abraham, 1809–1865—Family—Fiction.   4. Jews—United
States—Fiction.   5. Illinois—History—20th century—Fiction.]   I. Title.
PZ7.B735987My 2010   [Fic]—dc22   2009024151

First edition—2010 / Designed by April Ward
Printed in May 2010 in the United States of America by
R. R. Donnelley & Sons Company, Harrisonburg, Virginia

3   5   7   9   10   8   6   4   2

*For Hannah, who saved my life,
and my dad, AIB*

PART ONE

Love is the chain whereby to bind a child to its parents.

—ABRAHAM LINCOLN

My dad used to be Abraham Lincoln.

When I was six and learning to read, I saw his initials were A. B. E. Albert Baruch Edelman. ABE. That's when I knew.

My dad didn't look much like Lincoln—he was shorter and rounder, and he had a much bushier beard—but there was something about his eyes. Something watery and kind. Lincoln's soul staring out of my dad's face. My dad had a mole on his cheek, too—it wasn't on the same side as Lincoln's, and most of the time it was covered with hair, but it was enough of a sign.

I'm the one who suggested he name the furniture store Honest ABE's after he inherited it from his uncle David. People want to know the guy who sells them their beds and easy chairs is an honest sort, and we lived in the Land of Lincoln (a.k.a. Illinois), so people tended to go gaga over anything Abe-related. Plus David was dead, so the name David's Davenports was a little creepy. My older sister, Roberta, suggested Edelman's Fine Home Furnishings, which my mom liked but my dad thought was too snobby; the furniture he sold fell more into the "good, solid" camp than the "fine" one. My younger sister, Tabby, wanted him to call the store Jump on the Bed! Break Your Head! but Dad said his insurance company wouldn't go for it.

He ran with Honest ABE's. Business went up by 33 percent after he changed the name of the store, even though he kept the same stock. My dad dressed up like Lincoln in all of his newspaper ads, a big stovepipe hat on his head, his beard trimmed enough so you could see his mole. Some of the copy was pretty corny—"You don't have to wait four score and seven years for a great deal!" and "Log cabin or White House—we furnish them all!"—but every time I opened the *Downers Grove Sun* and saw his quarter-page ad, it felt like a love letter written just to me.

My dad used the whole family in one of his campaigns. We went to an old-timey photo studio where they had racks and racks of prairie dresses and bonnets for the girls to wear and vests and long jackets for the men. Men could hold rifles if they wanted; women could hold baskets of flowers.

The photographers told you not to smile, but in the picture, Tabby is grinning like a moron. Roberta and Mom look suitably old-fashioned and dour. I look like a normal girl from 1966, my eyebrows just a little raised. The edge of my T-shirt collar pokes up inside the neckline of my dress, which kind of ruins the effect. Dad looks very presidential, standing up straight and proud, one hand on the back of my mom's chair, the other hand tucked between the buttons of his vest. He also looks like he might bust up laughing any second. We got a sepia copy of the picture to use in the ads and a tintype one with a heavy wood frame to put up on our wall at home. The tintype started fading right away. We look like ghosts, slowly disappearing into the metal. One day, there will just be a pewter-colored oval inside the frame and we'll all be gone for good.

The ad says "From my family to yours, Honest ABE will never sell you wrong."

It didn't occur to me that all of us were the Lincolns until I had to write a social studies report about them at the end of sixth grade. Even then, it didn't hit me right away. For one thing, the Lincolns had four boys; we had three girls. But then I started to think about all of their names. Robert: Roberta. Tad: Tabby. William: me, Wilhelmina, which means "determined guardian"—or, if you want to be more direct with the translation, "desire helmet." But people just call me Mina. We didn't have a dead sibling named Eddie as far as I knew—who in their right minds would name a baby Eddie Edelman?—but everything else was too much of a coincidence to ignore. Plus, the Lincolns had a cat named Tabby, and Tabby loves cats! We even have a cat, who I named Fido after the Lincoln's dog. And then I saw a picture of Willie Lincoln staring up at me from a library book, and I could swear I was looking into my own eyes. Willie was leaning against a table in his long suit jacket, arms and legs crossed, daring me to recognize my old life. It became crystal clear to me as I wrote my report. We were the Lincolns. The Edelmans were the Lincolns reincarnated. And it became my job to make sure history wouldn't repeat itself. It became my job to save us from our fate.

Mina Edelman

Mrs. Turner

Social Studies

Grade 6

Period 4

6/6/66 (Almost the sign of the Beast!)

(Final Paper of the School Year! Huzzah!)

Life with the Lincolns

Abraham Lincoln was not just our 16th president. He didn't just free the slaves and have a funny hat and show up on the penny and the five-dollar bill. He had a family, too!

Mary Todd Lincoln was his wife. She came from a fancy family in Kentucky. Her family didn't like Abe much. They thought he wasn't good enough for her. Well, he proved them wrong, didn't he?! He became president of the US of A! The best ever! She became first lady, but lots of people thought she spent too much money fixing up the White House and buying dresses.

Before that, they had four sons. The first son was born in a tavern in 1843. His name was Robert Todd Lincoln. He was a bit of a wet rag. (I'm sorry to use that kind of language, Mrs. Turner, but he really was. He was very serious and not much fun. He even sent his mom to the loony bin when he was a grown-up!)

Next born was Edward "Eddie" Baker Lincoln. He

died when he was three in 1850. His mom wrote a poem about him after he died. She called him a "meet blossom of heavenly love." I don't know what a "meet blossom" is. Maybe she meant a "meat blossom"?

Their favorite son, Willie (a.k.a. William Wallace Lincoln), was born in 1850. He was very smart and nice and handsome. He liked railroads and poems and animals. His mother thought he was a "peculiarly religious child."

His brother Tad (a.k.a. Thomas Lincoln) was born in 1853. Abe Lincoln named him Tad because he looked like a tadpole when he was born, a big head with a tiny body. Tad pretty much grew into a frog, too—he was always jumping all over the place! He was always causing trouble, like spraying guests with the fire hose and setting off the servant bells in the White House and stealing strawberries that were supposed to be for a state dinner. He even tied a bunch of goats to a kitchen chair and rode around on it in the East Room (and that's a fancy room)! They had moved to the White House when Willie was ten and Tad was eight. Before that, they lived in a house in Springfield, Illinois (our capital!).

Tad and Willie were best friends. They got into lots of mischief together. (Although Tad was usually the one to blame. Willie was a lot calmer than Tad, but Tad got him running around and carving into the furniture and sliding down the banisters and finger-painting on the walls and other enjoyable things like that.) Abe and Mary Todd Lincoln pretty much let them do what they wanted. One of Abe's friends said the boys "were absolutely unrestrained in their amusements" and that Lincoln was "the most indulgent parent I have ever known." The boys liked that, but people around them didn't always, especially when the boys fired toy cannons during meetings or threw people's papers around! A guy who worked with Abe said that " had they s___t in Lincoln's hat and rubbed it on his boots, he would have laughed and thought it smart." Except he didn't say "s___t"; he said the real swear! I didn't know people could swear back in the old days, did you, Mrs. Turner?

Then Willie got sick when he was twelve. When he died, everything changed. His mom went crazy. She wouldn't go in the room that he died in, and she hired fortune-teller ladies (called "mediums") to get the spirits of Willie and Eddie to talk to her. Sometimes she saw Willie's ghost sitting on the foot of her bed. Tad was very sad when Willie died, too, and never got back to his same fun and games. He did like to go to the theater, but then his dad was shot in one, so that was that!

Tad died when he was eighteen, and of course, his mom went even crazier. She got scared of fire and scared of being by herself, and she couldn't sleep and had to take pills. She bought tons of stuff and went into debt and carried thousands of dollars on her so she wouldn't feel poor.

After she started selling her clothes to pawnshops, Robert sent her to a trial. In ten minutes the jury called her insane and said she had to go to a nuthouse. Mary got out of there after a few months, and she traveled around for a little, but then she got sick and died. No happy ending for Mary Todd Lincoln! And then Robert, the most boring of all the Lincolns, lived until he was 82. That's not fair! But he lived in Chicago for a long time, so that's nice. My kind of town.

In conclusion, Abraham Lincoln's family was both full of fun and full of dying and sadness. And that's my report.

B-

Mina,
Mary Todd Lincoln most certainly did not mean "meat blossom." Please refrain from using slang and personal interjections in your schoolwork (as well as references to the devil). This is an informative report overall, but you neglected to include your sources.
—Mrs. Turner

Dear Mrs. Turner,
I was there. I was Willie (the favorite). Isn't that enough of a source for you? Besides, isn't the Avery Coonley School supposed to give children freedom to learn their own way (which, it seems to me, should also give children the freedom to write reports and bibliographies their own way)?
Sincerely, your reincarnated student,
Mina

Mina,

The Avery Coonley School is also supposed to provide a rigorous education, which includes learning how to prepare a proper bibliography. As for your reincarnation claim, this is Social Studies, not Prank-the-Teacher class. If you can pull together a bibliography before tomorrow, I can bring your grade up to a B. And no more mumbo jumbo.

—Mrs. Turner

I liked getting good grades, and I had a whole stack of library books in my room to cite, but I had more important things to worry about than bibliographies. They weren't mumbo jumbo, either. As far as I could tell, my three main tasks were:

1. Get through age 12 without dropping dead
2. Stop Mom from going crazy
3. Stop Dad from getting shot in the skull

Number 1 appeared to be the most important. If I could do Number 1, I wouldn't have to worry about Number 2, and I don't mean that in a bathroom way. Mom wouldn't go crazy if I stayed alive. And if I could do Number 1, I'd be around to protect my dad. No one else was going to do it for him. Not Mom, not Roberta, not Tabby. Not my dad himself, that was for sure. It was going to have to be me. I had to live up to my "determined guardian" name. And as soon as school was out for the summer, I was able to devote myself to it full time.

Avery Coonley had a summer program, but my parents didn't sign us up. They didn't sign us up for anything—no day camp or horseback riding or swimming lessons or any other summer activity in or around the village of Downers Grove. Roberta was going to start up at the Lucy Webb Hayes School of Nursing in Washington, DC, that September, and my parents wanted us to be able to spend the summer together as a family before she flew the coop. Not that it worked. Roberta didn't like to spend time with me and Tabby; we were too "immature," too "sweaty," too "busy," too "spoiled," too "messy," too "uncouth" for her tastes (and I put all of these in quotation marks because she really called us all of those words). And we didn't like to spend time with her, because she was too "boring," too "stuck-up," too "better than everyone," too "bossy" and "hoity-toity-be-doity" to appreciate our games. (And, I have to admit, those are mostly words I used. Tabby usually used words like "thtupid." Tabby, I should mention, has a lisp.)

Tabby also has a scar running down her mustache skin.

Not that she has a mustache—it's just the place a mustache would be if she was a boy. The place a mustache grew when she was Tad, feathery and light before he died. When she was born as Tabby, she had a cleft palate, a.k.a. a harelip. Her lip was split apart in the middle, a split that went right up to her nose. She looked scary when she was born, like a monster movie rabbit. (Maybe that's why they call it a harelip!) She had an operation, and they sewed her up, and then her lip looked like a Frankenstein baby's. It was mostly normal after that, except her lip has one point on top instead of two, and a wormy white line goes up her mustache skin like a zipper. For a long time, she said her *s*'s like *th*'s. She couldn't really say her *r*'s, either. But Tabby doesn't mind her scar. She likes her pointy lip. She thinks it makes her look like a can opener.

I think the other reason that my parents didn't sign us up for summer stuff was because they were worried about money. Avery Coonley is expensive. My mom's mom left a trust to pay for our schooling when she died, but it didn't include summer activities. My mom sometimes asked her dad for money—he had a lot of it. He and his wife lived in a big fancy apartment on Lake Shore Drive in Chicago, and they had three cars for the two of them (a red MG convertible, a white Cadillac DeVille, and an ice blue Lincoln Continental), but he didn't share it with us very often, especially since he hated my dad.

We spent most of our time at home that summer. My best friends were all away, visiting places like grandparents' houses and overnight camp and Europe, so Tabby was my main companion. Our house looked a little like the Lincolns' old house (meaning *our* old house) in Springfield—two stories, Colonial, white with green shutters. I wonder if that's why my parents chose it—maybe part of them knew they were Abe and Mary reincarnated. Plus our house was the Lexington from the Sears catalog, and Mary was born in Lexington, Kentucky. Surely that wasn't a coincidence.

Downers Grove was full of Sears houses. The Lexington, my mom was proud to announce to anyone who would listen, was the biggest Sears model in town, with nine rooms, including two sun porches that jutted out on either side of the house—one was our den; the other, our breakfast room. The Sears houses arrived in the early 1920s by train, 30,000 to 40,000 pieces each, not including nails, ready to be assembled. Almost as easy as Lincoln Logs. I liked going into the basement or the attic and seeing the blue part numbers stamped on the beams. I wondered whose hands nailed them together, what families lived under the roof before ours.

The pillars by the front door made our house look a bit like the White House, but it resembled the Springfield house even more. The Springfield house looked like it was furnished by Honest ABE's, though, and the Downers Grove house looked like it was furnished by an alien. My mom liked modern furniture, things with swoopy lines and bright colors, things mostly made in Denmark or New York. The style didn't really fit our old-fashioned house. It was like turning the crank on a jack-in-the-box and having a robot jump out instead of a clown. Not terrifying, but not what you'd expect to find.

If we got stir-crazy, we would go outside and play in our deep front yard dotted with dandelions and violets or our equally deep backyard that ended where the train tracks cut through a stand of oak trees. We could see the back of Anderson's Lumberyard across the tracks. Sometimes workers there would smile and wave at us; other times, they scowled as if we were disrupting their sawing and stacking.

Tabby and I rode our bikes into town, through the Main Street Cemetery, past the train station where a train once smashed into a wall. Sometimes we rode to Avery Coonley, even though we weren't signed up for anything. The school has a lot of grass, and the forest preserve is right there. It was fun to run around and eat our lunch (which I always packed for us—usually chicken-with-French-dressing sandwiches) under the maple trees. I loved to think of all the syrup moving slowly inside of those trunks. Every winter at school, the second-graders go out in the snow and tap the maples for sap (which doesn't taste like Log Cabin, not one bit). The year Tabby's class did it, she got sap all over her rabbit fur parka. Our mom wasn't very happy about that. She didn't like how Tabby and I always managed to get grass stains and rips and Ragú spills on everything. Plus, our hair wouldn't stay in barrettes, our faces wouldn't stay clean. Maybe it's because we used to be boys, and not stuck-up ones like Robert.

People make a big deal about the buildings at the school because they were designed by a guy who was a student of Frank Lloyd Wright. I didn't know why that should matter. If I got famous for something, it wasn't going to be because of who my teacher had been. Why should Mrs. Turner get all the credit? I had my own mind, even if it was a reincarnated one. The buildings were pretty, though—red brick, with archways and tile, all facing a reflecting pool in the middle of the courtyard. My favorite thing about the school was the sea horses. They're all over the place—on the walls, on statues, on signs. Mrs. Coonley thought the sea horse should be our symbol because it's little and delicate and beautiful and part of a big ocean neighborhood, and because it stands up straight and swims upward, and that's how our spirits should be. I imagined our spirits probably shot up when we died, but I doubted that's what she had in mind. I think she meant we should shoot for good grades. I wondered how my spirit got from Willie to me. Maybe it shot up and up and up to the stars when Willie died, and then came back down when my mom was pregnant, when I was just a little sea horse inside of her, waiting for my soul.

One day at the end of June, Tabby and I pedaled onto campus. The summer program kids were splashing in the pool and learning archery on the grass and trying out some new dance moves on the sidewalks—someone had brought a record player outside, hooked to a long extension cord. It was a muggy day; Tabby's hair, which is usually just a little bit curly, exploded from her head like a puffer fish. The bottoms of my feet were sweaty against my flip-flops. My bottom itself was hot and sore from all that riding. Some girls we knew waved as they strutted around to "These Boots Are Made for Walkin'" in their sea horse T-shirts. Some waved to us from the water. I felt very jealous. I wanted to learn the choreography or jump in the pool, but I knew I'd get in trouble if I tried to join in. Those types of things didn't bother Tabby. If she thought of it, she would jump right into the water with her clothes on.

That day, she was leading us toward a line of kids waiting for chocolate-covered ice cream bars—she was sure we could snag a couple—when an arrow zipped past my ear. It sounded like a race car zooming around a corner, or maybe the loudest wasp in the world. The stiff feathers on the back, bright and blue as toilet cleaner, grazed my cheek before the arrow plunged into an elm tree a few feet away. I whipped around to see where the arrow had come from. My neighbor Hollister Burgeron glared at me from across the yard, his bow still raised. With his short reddish hair and big ears, he looked like Peter Pan, but evil. I had never seen such a look of hate on his face before. It made a little chill run down my legs.

"Hollister Burgeron tried to kill me," I said to Tabby in awe. My heart started to hammer; my cheek started to burn. Hollister lived three doors down from us in a much smaller house, a house that looked like a little yellow fishing cabin. No two houses on our block looked alike—there were Victorian houses, large brick houses, ranch style houses, Tudor, Craftsman, all with big broad yards. Another Sears house, too—a bungalow, the Starlight. We used to play with Hollister and his younger brother a lot, but I hadn't seen them since school ended.

Tabby made a growling sound. She dropped her brown

Schwinn on the grass and ran toward Hollister. I watched him stand there, laughing at her, until she rammed into him with her head and knocked him to the ground. The bow snapped in half beneath them. Tabby sat on top of his stomach and started punching him in the sea horse, her hands like pistons.

"Get off of me, you freak!" Hollister yelled.

"Don't you kill my sister!" she yelled back. She was about to punch him in the face when a counselor, a teenage boy, pulled her from him by the elbow. I ran toward them to make sure Tabby wasn't going to get creamed.

"What's going on here?" the counselor asked. He was the kind of boy Roberta would like—he looked like he had just combed his thick blond hair.

"He tried to murder Mina!" Tabby shouted.

"What?" the counselor asked. But he wasn't addressing Hollister, who should have been the interrogation subject. He was addressing Tabby. He was probably wondering what "twied to moodoomina" meant.

"Hollister Burgeron shot an arrow at my head," I told him, out of breath. Hollister was still giving me the stink eye. It made my stomach curdle. "It scratched my cheek."

"That's a serious accusation," the counselor said, his teeth very white. Roberta would definitely like him; she liked people who look like ceramic versions of themselves. He touched my cheek, and a sharp jolt went down my body. He turned to Hollister and said, "Did you do this?"

"It slipped out of my bow the wrong way." Hollister looked defiant.

"See?" said the counselor. "It was just an accident." He ruffled Tabby's bloated hair and went back to help the other kids figure out how to shoot arrows the right way.

"That was no accident," I said to Hollister. "You tried to decapitate me!"

"Well, your dad made my mom cry," Hollister said through clenched teeth. His teeth weren't so white. He seemed to get a sudden sunburn all over his face.

Tabby started to laugh, but stopped herself.

"He said my dad shouldn't be in Vietnam."

"Your dad's there?" We played Vietnam with Hollister and his brother in their yard a lot. We crawled around on our bellies and pretended to shoot each other. Sometimes Hollister lay on top of me to save me from a grenade.

"He went two weeks ago." Hollister scrunched his face up, blinked his eyes. I closed my eyes so I wouldn't see him cry. I could suddenly smell the breath of the maple trees all around us. I hoped he could smell it, too—the sweet of it. I wondered what his dad smelled in Vietnam. All I could think of was the smell of Hollister's yard, a grassy dustiness. Jungles probably didn't smell like grassy dust. They probably smelled more like wet dirt, wet plants, like the inside of the Chicago Arboretum. Or maybe they smelled like animals, like the monkey house at Lincoln Park Zoo. I opened my eyes. I didn't know what to say to him.

"You better get some Mercurochrome for that cut," he told me. He picked up the broken bow and ran back to join his group.

The cut was shorter than I expected it to be, but deeper, when I looked at it in the mirror at home. I grabbed *The Better Homes and Gardens Family Medical Guide* from my nightstand drawer and dragged it into the bathroom. The first aid section is full of diagrams that show things like how to get a fish hook out of someone's finger, plus helpful words of advice such as if children swallow an open safety pin, you should feed them mashed potatoes. I found the wounds, cuts, and bruises section, but I wasn't sure if my cut qualified as a "small, minor cut," "a deep, extensive cut," or a "puncture wound."

"When was the last time we had a booster shot for tetanus?" I asked Tabby, who, based on my orders, was sitting on the counter, washing my cheek with a clean cloth, each stroke moving away from the wound as the book directed.

"We had shots before school," she said. *Tots before thcool.* Almost a year ago. Maybe I should get another, just in case some metal from the arrow made its way under my skin. If it was a puncture wound, I should for sure.

"Do you think I need stitches?" I asked. The book said deep cuts may need stitches to minimize scars. Always get medical aid, it said.

Tabby shook her head as she dabbed at my face.

"I don't want to get a scar on my face," I told her, and then I felt bad, since she has that mustache-skin scar. She didn't seem to notice. She covered my cut with a Band-Aid, then kissed the spot.

"Uck." She spit into the sink. "Band-Aids taste like *thoes*." I didn't want to know how she knew what *shoes* tasted like.

"Thanks for being my assistant," I told her as we opened the door. Roberta was right outside of it, waiting for the bathroom. She had curlers in her hair, her special scarf tied over them, with fake bangs snapped to the front. The bangs were almost the color of her hair, a dark brown (the only thing about her that looked like dad), but the texture was all wrong. It was like doll hair, shiny and thick and plasticky. Her own hair was more thin and dull. It wouldn't poof out from her forehead the way those bangs did; her own hair would lie flat. She wore the special scarf so she could go out with curlers on, but I don't think it fooled anyone.

"What happened to you?" she asked.

"I got shot with an arrow," I told her.

She rolled her eyes. "And Tabby helped bandage you?"

Tabby beamed proudly.

"I'm the nurse in the family," Roberta said, glancing at the medical book in my hands. "If you need first aid, you should come to me."

"You're not a nurse yet," I reminded her, but I wondered if I should take the Band-Aid off and get her opinion, anyway.

"I'm more qualified than *she* is." She gestured to Tabby, who stuck out her tongue and ran downstairs. Before I could ask Roberta whether or not she thought I needed stitches, she shut herself and her fake bangs in the bathroom.

When I was Willie, I died of what they called "bilious fever." Some people now say it was probably typhoid fever; others say malaria. It didn't matter which one. I was ready for both. And I knew better remedies than the ones Dr. Stone gave me when I was Willie—Peruvian bark, calomel, and jalap (whatever those are) every half hour if I was awake, along with blackberry cordials, which sound very nice but didn't help me any. Also rice water and beef tea (ick), cold cloths on the forehead (my mom still does that when I have a fever), and mustard plasters (which sound like something that would sting your eyes and nose and be hard to get off your skin).

I had begged my mom to buy *The Better Homes and Gardens Family Medical Guide* at the grocery store—there was a big stack of them by the Quisp cereal at the end of an aisle. I told her it was so we'd know what to do if one of us broke a leg or ate poison or cracked our heads open. I told her the health teacher at school told us to buy it. But really I just wanted to know what symptoms I should be looking out for.

These are the symptoms of typhoid fever (p. 43): fever, of course, plus headache, cough, a slow pulse, and apathy, which my dad says means that you don't care about anything and that's why people don't vote.

The symptoms of malaria (p. 70) are "a sense of feeling ill" (thanks, *Family Medical Guide*, that helps a lot!), fever, chills, delirium, sometimes coma, and a few other things, including the weirdest—black pee! The strangest color my pee has been is orange, after I took a new kind of vitamin. It looked like Easter egg dye.

The book is thick, like a Bible. It's covered with ivory vinyl, bumpy and wrinkled like elephant skin, and has a burgundy vinyl spine. The letters on the cover and the wand with snakes wrapped around it are stamped in gold. It weighs about as much as three bricks on a plate.

There's a drawing of typhoid germs inside, how they'd look under a microscope. The picture has a light green background, like celery; the germs are a darker green, like the inside of an avocado. They look like upside-down jellyfish falling through water, their tentacles waving. Sometimes I thought I could feel them, floating and flitting inside my blood, tickling the insides of my veins. I asked the pharmacist if I could buy some chloramphenicol and cortisone to have on hand, just in case—the book says that's what is most effective for *Salmonella typhi*—but he said I needed a prescription. Dr. Wisener wouldn't give me one. I tried to pretend I had all the symptoms. "I feel real apathetic and slow pulsing," I told him, and lolled on the examining table like I didn't care about anything in the world, but he just told me to get some fresh air.

There's a picture of malaria germs in the book, too. Make that malaria *parasites*. They're different from germs. They look like tiny eyeballs in the drawing—gray egg-shaped rings with coral-colored pupils inside. They get inside a human cell (the color of ham) and multiply, and then they split the cell open and spill into the blood. I hadn't felt malaria in me yet. I tried always to spray myself with OFF! before I went outside, just in case. I sprayed all my sheets, too. They smelled a little like the inside of a can, but I thought it should keep the malaria away. And I could always try to get some quinine if I had to.

Just because I died of typhoid or malaria when I was Willie didn't mean that's what I'd die from as Mina, though.

My chest had been hurting for a while, a dull ache behind my nipples, like rug burn when it's starting to wear off, but under my skin instead of on top of it. I had been worried about breast cancer—one of my nipples had a little lump under it, like a knot, but the book said breast cancer doesn't usually hurt, so I lay in my bed and looked up "chest pain."

My bed and Tabby's were pushed against one wall together, almost like one long skinny mattress but with a gap in between just wide enough for the wooden floor lamp with the round paper shade. We slept head to head so we could both use the lamplight to read. My brain was just a few inches from her brain when we slept. I think sometimes her dreams jumped into my skull. I could tell when it happened, because I woke up feeling restless and exhausted.

I was glad she wasn't there while I looked through the book. I didn't want to scare her, and the most likely cause of chest pain appeared to be something scary, indeed: angina. The book said "one must face the fact that a person who has angina pectoris may die unexpectedly and coronary artery disease is not only the most common cause of sudden death, but in perhaps 15 percent, sudden death is the first and only manifestation of the disease." At least I had some advance warning.

The book said nitroglycerin is "the sovereign remedy and should be used freely, and particularly before any effort or strain which is known by the patient to have brought on attacks in the past. These may include all sorts of stresses; from opening the garage door in the morning to giving an after-dinner speech, appearing in court, or sexual intercourse."

Most of those things didn't sound stressful to me—opening garage doors and giving an after-dinner speech actually sounded like fun—but I could barely even look at the last thing on the list. *That* sounded very stressful, indeed. Maybe I could skip it altogether in my life, thanks to angina. If I got married, I could tell my husband, "I'm sorry, I can't do it with you—I have angina." Or if someone tried to rape me, I could say, "You better not rape me, because I have angina, and you could end up with a murder charge and not just a rape charge. And appearing in court is one of the most stressful things you can do. Think about that for a moment." The guy would probably zip up his pants and run away. So maybe angina wasn't such a bad thing to have, after all. But I still didn't want to drop dead from it.

Tabby was spinning around in the living room when I came downstairs, her dress billowing out like a mushroom. She had scrunched her hair into pigtails that stuck out on the sides of her head. She stopped spinning and dropped to the floor on her back. Our cat, Fido, climbed on top of her stomach.

"Now *you're* spinning!" she said, and, I have to admit, I did feel a little dizzy.

"Do you want to go to the drugstore with me?" I asked Tabby.

"If you buy me candy." Her eyes looked crazy, glazed. I wondered what I looked like from her perspective. Maybe like someone in one of those rides that spin so fast, they push you back onto a cushion because of centripetal force. Or was it centrifugal? I always forgot school words in the summer. I plunked down on the floor next to her.

"I'm not buying candy," I said. "I'm buying medicine."

"Why?"

"I have angina." I had to tell her sooner or later.

"I have angina, too!" She lifted up her skirt and pointed to her Casper the Friendly Ghost underwear. Fido jumped off and ran out of the room.

"AN-gina, not VA-gina, you weirdo. I could have a heart attack any second." I pulled her skirt down over her tan legs. Her skin was so soft, it made me feel funny inside. "Are you coming with me or not?"

"No, I need to spin some more." *Thpin thome more.* She didn't seem too worried. She jumped to her feet and stumbled around like a drunk girl, crashing into the black Eames lounge chair and ottoman before she started to twirl again.

I sprayed myself with OFF! before I rode my bike to Herschel's Pharmacy. I could feel my heart pounding as I pedaled up Main Street. I pulled my bike off the sidewalk and sat down on the grass so my heart wouldn't have to work so hard. I yanked out some clover flowers by the roots and tied them into a chain until it was long enough to fit around my wrist. The stems got a little sweaty and bruised, and the flowers turned kind of raggedy, but I loved the bracelet. I guess everything is beautiful when you know you're going to die.

The bracelet slipped up and down my arm as I walked my bike the rest of the way to the pharmacy, then broke and fell off in front of the BG Grill. I almost picked it up, but decided to leave it for someone else to enjoy. The ants, maybe.

The pharmacist looked tired when he saw me. He pointed to the Band-Aid. "Is it leprosy today, Miss Edelman? A boil? Shingles, perhaps?"

"A bow-and-arrow incident," I said. I tried not to think about Hollister's face when he told me my dad made his mom cry.

"I imagine you need some salve, then?"

"Nitroglycerin, please." I looked at him and thought, *Those hands could save my life.*

"What? Are you planning to blow something up?"

"I'm planning to *not* blow something up," I said. That was the whole point—to not blow up my heart.

"Nitroglycerin is a component of dynamite," he said, his fuzzy white eyebrows pulled down close to his eyes. "How do I know you're not plotting to blow Downers Grove to smithereens?"

I was a bit flattered that he thought I was some sort of criminal mastermind. "I have angina, if you must know," I said.

"Angina." He shook his head and smiled a little. "A young girl like you?"

"I'm afraid so," I said.

"Do you have a prescription?" he asked.

"You can't buy it over the counter? What if people need

it fast? *One must face the fact that a person who has angina pectoris may die unexpectedly.*"

"We wouldn't want that." He pulled a lollipop out from under the counter. A thin disk of green wrapped in cellophane, the stick looped back around into the candy so there is no sharp end. A safety lollipop. "I think this has nitroglycerin in it," he said as he handed it to me.

"I wasn't born yesterday," I told him, but I took the candy, anyway. "I'll be back with a note from my doctor."

The lollipop was a disgusting lime flavor, the worst of all hard-candy flavors, in my opinion. I tried to enjoy it—what if it was the last thing I ever got to taste in my life?—but I should have saved it for Tabby. Aside from dark chocolate, she never met a candy she didn't like. If she asked me why my tongue was green when I got home, I'd have to tell her it was a side effect of the medicine. The flavor stayed sharp in my mouth as I pedaled home, counting each beat of my poor doomed heart.

"**M**ina Ballerina!" my dad yelled from the kitchen table when I walked through the door. He had the newspaper and a plate of cinnamon toast and gherkin pickles, his usual after-work snack, in front of him. I could smell the furniture store on his clothes under the vinegar and sugar in the air. "I was thinking we could all catch a show at the Tivoli tonight. What do you say?"

"I don't know," I said. I loved going to the movies, especially at the Tivoli, with its fancy carved ceilings that, according to my mom, look like Versailles. The Tivoli was the second theater in the whole country to show "talkie" movies, so it made Downers Grove kind of famous. It always made me feel a little famous to go there. But as a determined guardian, it was probably wise of me to keep my father out of theaters. The Tivoli didn't have a balcony, but you never know where that shot is going to come from—the third row, the lobby, an archery bow. And supposedly a ghost lives in the basement.

"*Endless Summer* is playing." He popped a gherkin in his mouth. "It's about surfing."

"Maybe we should sit this one out," I told my dad. "I'm a landlubber. And you get seasick."

"It's a chance for all of us to be together, Mina." My dad looked disappointed as he crunched into his toast. Sprinklings of cinnamon tumbled into his beard.

"Maybe it would be okay." I wondered if I could convince him to wear a helmet. And put a cookie sheet under his shirt.

"What happened to your cheek?" he asked as if he just noticed the Band-Aid.

"I got hit by an arrow. Hollister Burgeron tried to shoot me."

"Why, that little . . . " My dad looked like he wanted to hunt Hollister down and throttle him.

My heart started to pound, but I tried to remind myself that giving a speech didn't have to be stressful. "Daddy," I said, "Hollister said you made his mom cry."

My dad put down his slice of toast. "That was unfortunate."

"What did you do?"

"I told her I hoped her husband wouldn't come home in a body bag." He shook his head as if he couldn't believe his own mouth.

"Daddy!"

"I was out of line. You know how carried away I can get, Mina." He reached toward my cheek. I pulled my face away; I didn't want him to press on it with his gigantic thumb.

When my mom came home from the tennis club, she threw a fit. She grabbed my arm so hard, I could feel her fingerprints against my bone.

"Why didn't your father take you to the emergency room?" she demanded. "You might need stitches!" Her terry-cloth wrist band rubbed my chin as she peeled back the Band-Aid. I could smell a tangy antidehydration salt pellet on her breath. Each tennis court had machines full of the bright yellow things.

"Tabby didn't think I needed them," I said.

"And since when is Tabby a medical expert?" she asked, her plastic visor falling down over her eyes, her blond hair still hairspray-stiff above it. "This is your face we're talking about, Mina!"

She took me to the ER, where the doctor said I didn't need a stitch, but my mom, still in her tennis clothes, insisted he give me one anyway, just to be on the safe side. The needle hurt a lot more than the arrow had. I felt like I was being branded. I tried to wrangle a prescription for nitroglycerin from the doctor when my mom wasn't listening, but he laughed and told me I had a good strong heart. I suggested an EKG, but he just gave me a lollipop—at least this one was cherry-flavored—and sent us on our way.

We didn't go to the movie that night. Roberta went to a friend's house. Tabby and I played our own version of Yahtzee at the family room table, even though my cheek seared and throbbed and made it hard to concentrate.

We had our own version of all the board games—Monopoly was all about the Chance cards for us; Scrabble was all about the craziest words we could make up. Yahtzee mostly involved shaking the dice cup so hard, the dice flew up like popcorn. I could feel each rattle inside the thread in my face. My parents sat on the low black couch together, my mom looking at catalogs, my dad watching a Buddhist nun set herself on fire.

"Is that what people have to do to get attention these days?" He gestured wildly to the television. I could look at the flames for only a second, knowing a person was inside of them.

"I don't recommend it, Al," my mom said, not looking up from her catalog. She flipped a page. I could see a row of women dressed in winter coats.

"Don't set yourself on fire, Daddy!" Tabby shouted, dice cup hammering like a maraca in her hand.

"Don't worry, sweetie," my dad said. "I prefer Dr. Martin Luther King's method. Nonviolent civil disobedience."

My mom sighed and turned to a page of gloves. "You haven't been disobedient a day in your life," she said. She hated when he talked about how connected he was to Dr. King just because Honest ABE's had furnished his apartment. I don't know if it would be better or worse if she knew about his connection to Lincoln.

"I married you, didn't I?" My dad put an arm around her.

My mom slowly tipped her head onto his shoulder. "That was *me* being disobedient. That was *you* being lucky."

They sat like that for a while; their heads obscured the

TV from where I was sitting, but I could hear the news shift into a peppy Chrysler commercial. Then my dad said, "I hope Dr. King is enjoying his furniture," and my mom lifted her head again. A LeBaron zoomed between their faces.

That January, my dad had received an unexpected call from Saul, an old friend of his uncle David's. My dad always used a Yiddish accent for Saul's voice and threw in a few Yiddish words when he told the story.

"Al," Saul said. "*Boychik*. I need your help."

"What can I do you for, Saul?" My dad was always one to help his fellow man.

"Did you hear that Martin Luther King Jr. is moving to Chicago?"

"I did not hear that," my dad said. "That's wonderful news!"

"For you, maybe," Saul said. "He's moving into my building."

"The one on Sheridan?" my dad asked.

"No," said Saul. "The one on Hamlin." Hamlin was in Lawndale, a part of Chicago that used to be a Jewish ghetto.

"The dump?" my dad asked. He had grown up in that neighborhood. It had gotten a lot worse over the years.

"The dump," said Saul.

"Why is he moving into a dump?" my dad asked.

"I don't know," Saul said, "but I've got to spruce up the place before the *shvartzer* gets here next month. I don't want the newspapers calling me a bad landlord. Do you think you could lend me a hand?"

"I don't think you should be calling Dr. King 'the *shvartzer*'" my dad said, "but tell me what you need."

My dad ended up bringing a whole truckload of furniture to 1550 South Hamlin Drive. We were at the store when he loaded the truck with a plaid couch, a four-poster bed, a dining room set with ladder-back chairs.

"Just think," he said, slapping the seat of an ice blue velveteen recliner. "A Nobel Prize–winning *tuchis* is going to sit right here." Saul's Yiddishness must have rubbed off on him.

"His *tuchis* won a prize?" Tabby asked. She bounced on the seat a few times until my mom told her to stop, she'd ruin the springs. I touched each piece of furniture inside the sawdust-smelling truck, trying to send a little thought into the fabric and wood—"I hope you write a good speech on this table. . . . I hope you have good dreams in this bed."

My mom didn't let us go with my dad to deliver the furniture. She said the neighborhood in Lawndale was too dangerous. We would get mugged, and that was only if we were lucky.

I worried about my dad all day. He shouldn't go into dangerous neighborhoods, not with his history of getting shot. But he didn't get mugged or killed or anything. He didn't get to meet Dr. King, either, much to his disappointment. Dr. King hadn't arrived in Chicago yet.

"The place was a zoo," my dad said after he got back. Our kitchen was filled with the smell of pot roast. "Electricians, plumbers, painters. Saul is going all out to get the place ready."

"Of course he is," my mom said. She helped him take off his bulky coat, unwrapped the tartan scarf from his neck. "He has a VIP tenant coming. I'd be on my knees waxing the floor, myself."

"Now that's something I'd like to see." My dad slapped my mom on the rear; his padded glove made a funny thwack against her wool skirt. She yelped a little, then smiled as she pulled the gloves off his hands. My mom was not the floor-waxing type. The cleaning lady took care of stuff like that.

"Seriously, Margaret," he said, opening and closing his naked fingers to get the cold out of his joints. "The whole neighborhood could use some sprucing up. It's a sad state of affairs. All the kids have runny noses. There's nowhere for them to run around. At least when I lived in the neighborhood, we had room to play stickball."

"So why is Dr. King moving there?" she asked. "You would think he could afford something nicer. He must make a pretty penny on speaking engagements by now." My mom thought every penny was pretty. Quarters were even prettier. Paper money was positively gorgeous.

"Saul seems to think it's just to make him look bad," my dad said.

"Oh, yes." My mom lifted the lid on the pot of potatoes. Starchy heat filled the room. "Martin Luther King Jr. is coming all the way to Chicago to make Saul Abromowitz look bad."

"Saul's owned that building for forty years. He's seen a lot of changes."

"Some things never change." My mom jabbed a fork into

the potatoes to see if they were tender. She held out a steaming morsel for my dad to taste. He opened his mouth. "I'll bet this is the first time he's painted those walls in forty years. The cheapskate."

"Anyway." My dad grimaced before he swallowed. The potato must have been hot. "I imagine Dr. King has family there. I don't know why else he'd want to live in such a godforsaken place."

"Family can make you do crazy things," my mom said. She poured the potatoes into a colander in the sink. So much steam billowed up, I couldn't see the expression on her face.

That was about half a year ago, but sometimes my mom still seemed to have steam around her head. I could almost feel it rising off her as she sat stiffly next to my dad on the couch, Johnny Carson on TV now. Dice flew all over the room when Tabby shook the Yahtzee cup. One must have bounced off my mom's hair; I saw her lift her hand to the top of her bouffant hairdo. Tabby was lucky our mother used so much hairspray; otherwise, she'd be in big trouble.

"You better pick those up," I said. My cheek throbbed. I was worried my stitch would pop.

"Nah," she said. "I'm going to bed."

"Tabby . . . ," I started, but she ran away. I stalked around the room, picking up the little cubes. It took almost twenty minutes to find them all. My parents turned off the TV before I was done. When I got to our room, Tabby was snoring. I slipped the dice inside the waistband of her nylon pajama bottoms, but then I couldn't fall asleep. I was worried she might get internal bleeding if she rolled on top of them and they pressed into her vital organs. I reached back into her pajamas and pulled them out again; they were warm, like little coals. She barely stirred. I put the dice on my stomach to feel the squares of heat against my own skin before I plunked them back into their cup.

"Let's go visit Dad at the store," I said to Tabby in the morning. I wanted to give my heart a rest, and the store seemed like the perfect place to avoid bows and arrows and bicycle races.

We spent the day digging into the cushions of the armchairs and poking our heads under dressers and opening all the drawers of the china hutches—we found six dimes, three quarters, and twelve pennies that way, plus a matchbook and a guitar pick and something that looked like a pile of cracker crumbs. Tabby tasted them, though, and said they were probably vanilla wafer crumbs. Vanilla wafers with something gross added to them, like soap. I told her she shouldn't eat stuff she found in furniture. I also told her that she shouldn't jump from bed to bed—she might break a bed frame, or even a bone—but she just laughed. And our dad said it was fine for her to have some fun, as long as customers weren't in the store. But most of the time, customers were there. Our dad hovered over them and explained the construction of the furniture and helped them look through big books to see which types of wood or upholstery or drawer pull would look best inside their houses. He was like a movie star with the customers, charming and very persuasive in his little spotlight. They all looked to him as if he had all the answers of the world. At least the world of home furnishing. And he pretty much did. Almost no one left without buying something, even if it was just a lampshade or a bottle of lemon-scented furniture polish.

I loved being at the store. I loved the smell of all the wood. I loved looking at all of the fabric swatches in my dad's desk drawers, running my hands over the different textures, imagining which ones I would choose if I had my own house. When I grew up, I decided, if I grew up, I wanted all puffy furniture. Nothing like the sleek stuff at home. I would choose velveteen and corduroy and pillows filled with feathers.

I wished I could do something to help my dad at the store, but he did such a good job on his own, I wasn't sure what I could add. He took care of customers, and his secretary, Phyllis, did all of the filing and the dusting and everything else that was related to tidying. I could have offered to help her, but those tasks didn't seem like much fun. So I decided to start a little newspaper for the store. I would call it the *Lincoln Log* and would include information about furniture and Abe. I knew my still-unreturned-even-though-it-was-summer-and-I-was-racking-up-huge-fines Lincoln library books had a few tidbits about furniture inside. When

Tabby and I got home, I pored through them, waiting for words like *chair* and *bed* to pop out at me. I copied down what I found, wrote it up into columns, and brought the page to the store the next day, where Phyllis typed it up for me.

When I showed the paper to my dad, he liked it, but he thought I should include some more information about the store itself. I made a few notes in the margins and Phyllis typed it up for me again.

THE LINCOLN LOG
AN HONEST ABE'S PUBLICATION

Issue 1

Mina Edelman, Editor in Chief

Tabby Edelman, Assistant Editor

Albert Edelman, Consultant

SOME LINCOLN FURNITURE FACTS THAT YOU PROBABLY NEVER KNEW

The very first piece of furniture Abraham Lincoln ever laid eyes on was a chest of drawers his dad brought home when Abe was nine. Nine, and he had never seen furniture before! It's almost hard to believe. Can you imagine not ever seeing a bed? Don't worry, though! You can see lots of beds and any other furniture you like at Honest ABE's!

Here is a description of Lincoln's law office, from a guy who was a clerk there:

"The furniture, somewhat dilapidated, consisted of one small desk and a table, a sofa or lounge with a raised head at one end, and a half-dozen plain wooden chairs. The floor was never scrubbed. . . . Over the desk a few shelves had been enclosed; this was the office bookcase holding a set of Blackstone, Kent's Commentaries, Chitty's Pleadings, and a few other books."

Honest ABE's furniture is never dilapidated. Plus, the floor is usually clean! I would like to know what Chitty was pleading about, wouldn't you? Do you think he's related to Chitty Chitty Bang Bang?

When the Lincolns left Springfield to go to the White House, they auctioned off most of their furniture. A lot of it ended up in Chicago and burned in the Great Chicago Fire, but you can still see some of it if you go to the Lincolns' house in Springfield. I would say that it's not as nice as the furniture at Honest ABE's, though!

The day Lincoln died, a bunch of people went to the boardinghouse where he was taken after he got shot and they cut off pieces of the bloody sheet and carpet for souvenirs! Pretty gross. The bed in the room there was way too little for Abe, but at least he got to lie in a bed, unlike in his floor-sleeping childhood. That's sort of an improvement, in a way, except for the fact that he died.

When Mary Lincoln was taken off to the nuthouse, she packed up a bag full of footstools, but no one knows why. I guess she really was crazy. Just like you'll be crazy about our furniture! Honest ABE's might even have a footstool for all of your foot-resting (or nuthouse) needs.

THANK YOU FOR READING <u>THE LINCOLN LOG</u>!

We ran off sixty copies on the copy machine in the office and left the stack, hot and smelling wonderfully of ink, on an end table just inside the door. Seeing my name in purplish print made me feel important and proud. Even if I did die, at least someone could look at that piece of paper and say "Wow. She was an editor in chief at twelve years old." It could be my legacy. I think my dad was happy with the extra advertising, although he said we probably shouldn't imply that some of our customers need to go to the nuthouse.

As assistant editor, Tabby was supposed to draw a wooden log on the top of every page, but after she got through seven loggish shapes, she started to draw logs with fangs and creepy eyes and hair, and I told her that her work was done. She seemed relieved. I wanted to throw her pages away, but I couldn't bring myself to do it. It would feel like throwing away her scar. I slipped those pages to the bottom of the stack instead and hoped they wouldn't scare anyone too badly. They didn't seem to. We only heard good things about the *Log*.

For the Fourth of July, we ran off even more copies. My dad dressed up like Lincoln, and I tied a Colonial bonnet under my chin (even though I would have rather worn a Willie suit) and we walked along the edge of the parade route, passing out free copies to everyone sitting on the curb. It was good publicity for Honest ABE's, plus more people would know my name before my obituary showed up. Everyone seemed happy enough to see us, although I did see a lot of *Log*s on the ground after the parade was over. My dad stayed dressed like his old self past the parade, past the barbecue and the cakewalk, all the way into the night when we sat on the grass at Avery Coonley and watched the fireworks. Fireflies made their own light show closer to the ground; Tabby and I chased them around for a while before I curled up on my dad's lap, one firefly cupped between my hands. I could feel my dad's stovepipe hat tower above us, feel his beard press into the top of my head, as light seeped soft through my fingers, like Willie still glowing inside me.

At dinner a few days later, his mouth full of green bean almondine, my dad said, "I have to go to a furniture convention in Chicago tomorrow, and I thought I'd take Mina."

"What sort of furniture convention?" My mom perked up. She was cutting her roast chicken into teeny tiny pieces, as if she were trying to break it down to its molecular structure. The skin lay on the side of the plate like a discarded raincoat.

"Nothing you'd be interested in," my dad said. "It's a closeout thing. Remainders. Floor models. Good deals from the manufacturers I already work with." He winked at me. My mom sighed and went back to her chicken disassembling.

"I wanna go!" Tabby said. She had given her dinner roll a green bean wig. It looked like a sea monster.

"Sorry, kiddo." My dad ruffled her hair. "You have to be at least ten to get in. And Mina's been interested in the furniture business lately. Haven't you, Mina?"

"I guess so," I said.

"The *Lincoln Log* is a great hit with the customers. Maybe we could convince the manufacturers to distribute it—"

"It's very store specific, Al," my mom said. "I don't think it would be of interest to the manufacturers."

I felt as if my mom had kicked me in the ribs, but her feet were still neatly folded under her chair.

"Not that it isn't interesting, honey." She touched my hand. "I think it's wonderful. It just has a limited audience."

"Well, maybe this convention will inspire her to increase her audience," my dad said. He stared at my mom until she coughed.

"I hope this doesn't mean I have to watch Tabby all day," Roberta said, across the table from me and Tabby. She was involved in the same careful chicken dissection as my mom. "I'm supposed to go shopping with Dorothy."

"Your mother should be here tomorrow," my dad said. "Isn't that right, Margaret?"

My mom cleared her throat and smoothed her napkin on her lap. "I had some plans," she said, "but I can reschedule."

"Well, then." My dad beamed at me.

Chicago was only about twenty-five miles away, but it felt like a different planet. If Downers Grove was a TV show,

Chicago was a movie—bigger and louder, with a much larger cast. Color on a movie screen is much more vivid than color on a TV screen, because you can see more of it spread out all over the place. I loved going there, but I always felt like people would know I was just a TV girl.

My dad's car smelled like old smoke and salami and sweat. Man smells. My mom's car smelled like perfume and hairspray. I didn't get to sit in the front seat of either car very often, and I felt very grown-up so close to the dashboard. I rubbed my head back and forth against the vinyl seat until my hair stood up from the static. My dad smiled at me and pushed in the cigarette lighter. I could smell the burnt metal heat of it right away, different from the damp green heat outside. When he pulled it out, the hot orange coil was beautiful, a glowing ring of Saturn.

We were halfway to Chicago when my dad made his confession. "I should tell you, Mina," he said, "we're not going to a furniture convention."

"We're not?" I was disappointed. I had brought a notebook and worn my most reporterlike clothes: tan pants, a white short-sleeved button-down shirt, and one of my dad's fedoras, with a handmade PRESS card in the band, a sock bunched inside so it wouldn't slip down over my eyes. The only part of me that didn't feel official was my sandals, but I doubted too many people would look at my feet. I was excited by the prospect of expanding my *Lincoln Log* audience. I wanted to interview all the manufacturers about how they made their furniture. It could be a new column— "Furniture Factory Facts." Maybe "Furniture Fact-ories."

"We're going someplace better," he said. "But I didn't want anyone else to know."

My mind reeled with possibilities—the Shedd Aquarium, the Adler Planetarium, maybe the miniature rooms at the Art Institute. Tabby would be so jealous if I got to go to a museum without her. Except the Field Museum. She hated the dead animals there, stuffed in glass cases. If my dad took me to the Field Museum alone, she wouldn't get too mad.

"We're going to see Dr. Martin Luther King Jr.," he said. I hadn't considered that as a possibility. "He's giving a speech at Soldier Field."

We had gone to see the Bears play there once. I hated the game, but we went to the Museum of Science and Industry and watched chicks hatch in the incubator afterward, so the day wasn't a complete loss. "He's not going to talk about football, is he?"

"I doubt it." My dad laughed and squeezed my shoulder. "I hope we'll get a chance to talk to him. I'm dying to know how he likes the furniture."

I wanted to tell my dad to turn the car around right then and there. A conversation about furniture wasn't worth dying for. And a stadium was like a big theater; it could be full of potential Booths. But then my dad said, "I'm glad you're coming with me, Mina," and I didn't want to disappoint him. I would just have to be extravigilant.

Soldier Field was brimming with thousands of people—mostly colored, but a few white people, too. Everyone seemed very excited. I left my fedora in the car—it was a hot day and the hat made my head sweat too much—but the sun was so bright, my dad bought us a couple of straw hats from a vendor so we could have a little shade. We climbed into the stands and found seats high up in the nosebleed section. I was a little worried when my dad called it that. I kept putting my finger under my nose to check for blood—you can die if your nose bleeds too much because it means it's coming from your brain—but luckily my finger came back clean. Some singers I hadn't heard of before sang—my dad was especially thrilled about Mahalia Jackson—and some people I hadn't heard of before said a few words, and then Archbishop Cody introduced Dr. Martin Luther King Jr.

As Dr. King's Cadillac drove onto the field, the crowd went wild. My dad couldn't contain himself. He turned to the man next to us, and said, over all the hooting and hollering, "I furnished his apartment."

The man stared at my dad for a second in disbelief. Then a laugh came out of his throat, sharp, like a gunshot. I grabbed my dad's arm.

"You're the crazy cracker who did that?" the man asked.

"The one and only," my dad said, rocking on his heels, proud.

"Man." The man laughed again and shook his head. "What'd you go and do that for?"

My dad looked at the man incredulously. "I wanted him to feel welcome," he said.

"He gave all that furniture away," the man said. "It's scattered all over the neighborhood."

"What?" my dad asked. I could see the air deflate from his lungs.

"Dr. King came to Chicago to prove a point, and you ain't helped him any. He wanted to show the world how bad the slums were. How's he gonna show that when there's fresh paint on the walls and new furniture in every room?"

"I thought I was helping. . . ." My dad's chest caved in. He seemed to get smaller and smaller by the second.

"Are you with Mayor Daley?" the man asked, his face clouding with suspicion. I wondered if he could be dangerous. I glanced at his pockets. No sign of a gun or knife. But if he made a quick move, I was ready to jump in front of my dad, push him out of the way.

"That blowhard?" my dad said, indignant. "What do you take me for?"

"Daley's trying to stop us at every turn," the man said. "It wouldn't surprise me if he tried to pretty up them buildings before the news cameras came."

"Mayor Daley had nothing to do with it," my dad said. "A friend of the family asked me for furniture, I brought furniture. And I was glad to do it. I'd do anything for Dr. King."

The man sighed. "Well, at least that furniture went to people who needed it," he said. "My cousin got the davenport. It's his baby boy's bed now."

My dad looked as if he might cry.

A woman selling ice cream bars edged up the concrete steps. I wondered if the metal box was cold against her stomach. It looked heavy—the canvas straps were digging into her shoulders.

"Can I get one, Dad?" I asked. He turned around, surprised, as if he had forgotten I was there.

"Of course, Mina Ballerina," he said. He seemed rattled as he dug in his pocket for his wallet. "What flavor would you like?"

"We only got coconut left," the woman said.

"Coconut's great," I said, even though I would have preferred strawberry. Coconut sometimes made my throat itch. And it felt like cuticles in my mouth.

"I can't believe he gave the furniture away," my dad said under his breath as he looked wistfully out at the field. He had seen the furniture as his connection to greatness, and now that connection was gone. I could have told him not to worry, he was the great Abe Lincoln, but it didn't seem the right time or place. Not with so many people around. His forehead was beaded with sweat.

"You know what, though, Mina?" he said, more determination in his voice. "This gives me a chance to have an even deeper bond with Dr. King. Not just furniture—now I can help him do the real work."

Before I could ask him what he meant, Dr. King got out of the car and the crowd went crazier, making it too loud to talk. All that yelling seemed to make the air even more hot. As soon as I peeled off the wrapper, my ice cream started to drip down the stick, onto my wrist. My dad unbuttoned his collar.

Even though Dr. King looked the size of a doll from where we were standing, his voice was like God's, big and booming and everywhere. "We are here because we are tired," he said, and the crowd quieted down so they could hear every word that came out of his mouth. I tried to pay attention—I was tired, just like him, and wanted to know what to do about it—but between the melting ice cream and keeping an eye on the man next to my dad and the crowd in general, my brain was too full. Then Dr. King said, "We must declare our own emancipation proclamation," and my brain perked up. I looked at my dad to see if there was any glimmer of recognition—Dr. King was saying his words!—but he just looked pale and clammy and miserable. When Dr. King went on to say that we need to "make any sacrifices necessary to change Chicago," my dad's knees buckled. His eyes rolled back in his head. He crumpled like a tissue, toppling onto the people in the row below us.

"Daddy!" I screamed.

The crowd closed in around him.

"Daddy!" I screamed again. Four colored men hoisted him into the air.

"Leave him alone!" I yelled. "Put him down!" I could see the sweat pasting his shirt to his body. No blood. No bullet holes that I could tell. But maybe one was hidden somewhere.

The men started carrying him down the steps. I ran after them, dizzy and frantic. My foot was wet, and I wondered if maybe I was bleeding—maybe I had been shot, too—but then I realized I had dropped my ice cream onto my sandal.

"Heatstroke," I heard someone say. But I knew better. I knew someone had hurt him. How could I have let this happen? I should have told him to turn the car around when we had the chance.

"Put him down!" I kept yelling.

"Our power does not reside in Molotov cocktails, rifles, knives, and bricks," I heard Dr. King say. He got larger and larger as I rushed down the steps, dodging people's arms and legs, keeping an eye on my dad's bouncing hair. Were the men going to take my dad onto the field? Were they going to make some sort of example of him, of what could happen to white people if they weren't careful? I hoped they heard what Dr. King just said about not using weapons.

My dad came to when we were still thumping down the steps. "What in the—," he shouted, twisting his head around. "Mina? Mina!"

"I'm here, Daddy!" I called out, so relieved to hear his voice. "I'm right behind you!"

"You passed out, man," one of the men carrying him said. "We're going to get you some help."

A medical tent had been set up near the field. A lot of people were lying on their backs on the concrete, cool cloths over their heads. Women in nurses' uniforms were handing out paper cups of water and the little yellow salt tablets that my mom always sucked out on the tennis court. "Welcome to heatstroke central," one of them said.

The men lowered my dad to the ground.

"Are you okay, Daddy?" I knelt down next to him and did a quick scan for any possible bullet holes. He looked awfully pale. A sign of blood loss?

"I'm a new man," he said with a weak smile.

"You take it easy, sir," one of the men said. Another lifted his straw hat.

"Thank you for your kindness," my dad said. "I hope I didn't throw any of your backs out."

As the men laughed it off, I realized that one of them was the man who had been standing next to my dad. "Don't you go and do anything else crazy now," he said before heading back to the stands.

From the medical tent, we had a great view of the field. I could see Dr. King perfectly. His lips were like pillows. His suit was so dark and crisp. I imagined he must be hot in a dark suit in the sun. Someone else must have thought so, too; they held an umbrella over his head. But he didn't look hot. He stood tall and straight and talked as if he was as cool and comfortable as could be. About a million microphones rose up around the podium, which had been draped with an American flag. They bent toward him like silver tentacles, an octopus ready to swallow him up. But he wasn't going to let that happen—he wasn't going to get angina from public speaking, either, that was for sure. A big red and white circle sign stood in front of the podium—the circle had a red line across it like a belt, with a V on top of the line.

"What does that sign mean, Daddy?" I asked. My dad was sitting up now, a cool cloth pressed to the back of his neck.

"I don't know, Mina," he said. "Maybe one of these lovely ladies could clue you in."

"It's for the Chicago Freedom Movement," the nurse taking his pulse said, her fingers light on his wrist. Her dark skin made his skin look even more pale.

"Did you feel my heart leap?" my dad asked her. "Because that's my movement now, too."

She smiled and moved on to her next patient. I wondered if I should pull her aside when she was done, ask her about my angina.

"So let us all, white and black alike, see that we are tied in a single garment of destiny," Dr. King said. "We need each other."

"We do." My dad nodded. "We do."

I need you, Daddy, I wanted to say. I need you to not die. Everything else—this field, all these people, this one man they've all come to hear—didn't matter to me.

"Things are going to be different from now on, Mina." When my dad looked at me, I noticed something new in his eyes. Something burning and alive. A little scary. "My head is out of the sand for good."

Sometimes, when we went to the beach, Tabby and I took turns burying each other in the wet sand by Lake Michigan. I liked the heavy weight of it on my skin, but I don't think I'd want it over my head. It always felt good to break through that thick damp blanket and shake away the extra grains and feel the sun on my body again. Maybe that's how it felt to wake up from a faint.

Dr. King's voice reverberated as he said, "I'm still convinced there's nothing more powerful to dramatize a social evil than the tramp tramp of marching people."

My dad jumped to his feet. He wavered a little, and I thought he was going to tip over again, but he gained his footing, grabbed my hand, and said, "Let's get tramping, then."

Dr. King started a procession to City Hall. Because we were down near the field, we got to be up near the front of the group. Dr. King's Cadillac led the way. It was a wild sea of people, filling the street curb to curb. I was worried my dad would fall again, but he was in his glory, chanting "hey hey ho ho, Mayor Daley's got to go" along with the rest of the crowd, and singing "We Shall Overcome" and "Amazing Grace," which I didn't even know a Jewish person was allowed to sing. Lots of people had signs—things like END MODERN SLAVERY—DESTROY DALEY MACHINE and OPEN UP CHICAGO and HATE COSTS TOO MUCH! One guy had a sign full of smooshed words that said DON'T HATE THE WHITE; DON'T BE ANTIWHITE OR POOR WHITE TRASH; BE PRO-AMERICAN; VOTE FOR GEORGE C. WALLACE IN 1968, but some people tore it out of his hands and ripped it up and told him to go home. It was a little scary, but no one tried to hurt anyone, just the cardboard. My dad told me that George C. Wallace was the governor of Alabama and wanted to keep black people and white people apart. The guy with the sign should have known that people out to see Dr. King wouldn't like it.

We marched for blocks and blocks. My dad kept going as if he had never passed out. He looked as if he could march forever, as if someone had turned a crank on his back. My ice cream sandal was sticky. My foot was welded to it, but every once in a while, a toe would peel away and startle me. I wanted to run to the lake and dunk my feet in it.

Six men walked in a group, two rows of three carrying planks on their shoulders that held a big liberty bell in the middle. They looked like the people who carry coffins outside after a funeral, but they didn't look sad. Hot and tired, maybe sore from the carrying, but not sad. Everyone had a very determined look on their face, the kind of look Tabby gets when she's trying to explain something to someone. Focused and ready to burst with frustration and excitement.

When City Hall came into view, Dr. King and some other people got out of the Cadillac. Dr. King hoisted a small boy on his shoulders. My dad said it was his son. I would have liked to have seen what the boy could see from up there over his dad's head. Probably thousands of people, most of them in hats of all colors and shapes, surging down the street toward us. I wished I still had on my dad's fedora with the fake PRESS card, and not the silly itchy straw hat we bought in the stands. With a fedora I would look more like the important people. The straw hat made me feel like a scarecrow. A circle of people formed to protect Dr. King as he stepped up to the door of the building. I couldn't see anything after that—so many people pushed forward. My dad wrapped an arm around me to protect me from the throng. Someone's elbow pushed into my ear. Someone's shoe stepped on my heel. My straw hat teetered and tottered on my head.

"Stay with me, Mina," my dad said, pulling me closer to

him. I could smell the sweat and lunch of everyone around me. Lots of oniony stink. I tried not to get too claustrophobic or queasy from it. My dad offered commentary about what was happening with Dr. King. "He's unrolling a scroll," he said. "He's taking out a roll of tape. He's taping the scroll to the door. My God, he's just like Martin Luther, isn't he, Mina? Putting his demands on the door like that."

"He *is* Martin Luther," I reminded him.

"Not the one who lived hundreds of years ago," my dad said. "That was Martin Luther of the Lutherans. Dr. King is Martin Luther of the Baptists, I believe."

I wished I knew as much as my dad.

"And he's the Martin Luther of all of us, too—right, Dad?" I asked. "Even the Jewish ones? Or the semi-Jewish ones?"

"That he is, Mina." My dad smiled at me and squeezed me so hard, my straw hat almost tumbled right onto LaSalle Street.

We didn't get to see what was written on the scroll Dr. King taped to the door. Too many people rushed to take a look, and my dad started to get a little dizzy again, so we squeezed sideways through the crowd, walked over a couple of blocks, and hailed a cab to take us back to our car at Soldier Field. I saw the list in the paper the next day, though. There were demands for real estate boards to make all houses available to all people, demands to banks to give loans to everyone, demands to the mayor and political parties and the housing authority and businesses and unions and the governor and the federal government and the Cook County Department of Public Aid, all of them having to do with making life more fair. There were demands for "people," too. They were:

1. Financial support of the Freedom Movement.
2. Selective buying campaigns against businesses that boycott the products of Negro-owned companies.
3. Participation in the Freedom Movement target campaigns for this summer, including volunteer services and membership in one of the Freedom Movement Organizations.

My dad tapped the paper right on the people section of the demands. He leaned over and whispered in my ear, "We can do all three of those things, Mina." It made me feel more qualified to be a person than ever.

I wasn't supposed to tell my mom or my sisters anything about going to the rally or the march with my dad. They still thought we had gone to a furniture convention. I had to lie about how much fun it was to learn about dovetail joinery and upholstery piping (my dad coached me on all the correct words on the way home). I was a little nervous about how such lying, especially to Tabby, could affect my heart, but when my dad winked at me, it all seemed worthwhile. This was an important secret. We didn't want anyone to worry about us as we tried to change the world. Not that I could stop myself—worrying about us seemed to be my main hobby.

I wondered what sort of demands each member of my

family would tape to a door. My mom's would probably be "Money, please!" Roberta's would probably be "Treat me like a big shot or leave me alone!" Tabby's would be "Play with me!" My dad's would be something like "Listen to Dr. King and make life fair. And buy my furniture." I wanted to think mine would be something that would help everyone like that, but if I had to be honest with myself, it would probably be something more like "Please don't kill me or my dad." Addressed to both germs and people.

Even with our straw hats, my dad and I both got sunburned from our time at Soldier Field. My dad's face was especially red. He even got a few blisters that popped and sent clear liquid dribbling down his cheeks. As I peeled skin off my forearms, my mom said, "I don't see how you could get sunburned at a furniture convention. Are you sure the two of you didn't run off to Boca Raton for the day?" My heart was pounding a million miles a second, but I said, "It was outside. You need to take furniture outside to breathe every once in a while, you know."

My mom gave me a funny look. "I wasn't aware of that," she said. Later that day, I noticed the Eames chair was in the backyard, the black leather soaking up the sun, and I felt both awful and a little giddy that she had believed me. I hoped leather couldn't get a sunburn like any other type of skin.

That Tuesday at the breakfast table, my dad said, "Mina, I have another meeting with a manufacturer in Chicago today. Do you want to join me?"

"Don't you have to be at the store?" my mother asked as she poured milk into his cereal bowl. He rarely spent week-days away from Honest ABE's.

"The meeting isn't until the evening," my dad said. "And Phyllis can mind the store if I leave a little early."

"I'll mind the store, Daddy," Tabby said, her mouth full of Rice Krispies.

"I think you're a bit young, sweetheart," my dad said. "But Roberta is old enough. Is that something you'd be interested in, honey? Holding the reins of the store for a few hours?"

"I have plans today," Roberta said with a huff. "Besides, I'm not interested in retail."

"Other than the shopping end of it, of course." My mom smiled and tapped some Taster's Choice granules into her coffee cup.

"Furniture isn't my thing, Daddy," Roberta said. "I thought you knew that."

"Well, it may surprise you to learn that furniture isn't my thing, either," my dad said.

My mom gave him a sly smile as if to say that she knew that *she* was his thing. He smiled back and squeezed her hand. Then he said, "Justice is my thing now," and she slammed the coffee container down so hard, little brown flecks rained all over the glass tabletop. It made the air smell wonderful. I wondered how something that smelled so good could taste so awful. Tabby liked coffee for some reason. She pressed her finger onto some of the shiny pieces and licked them off. My mom pushed her chair away from the table and went to get a wet dishrag.

I wondered if my dad was going to say something about the real meeting in Chicago. If he was going to talk about justice, maybe he would start talking about Dr. King, too, but he only said, "I better get ready for work. Thanks for breakfast, Margie." My mom didn't answer. She just pushed the rag over the table, sending brown streaks across the glass.

I wore my reporter's outfit again that evening—my mom hadn't had a chance to wash it yet, so it was a bit wrinkled and smelly, taken straight from the hamper. I hoped I'd be able to interview a few people. That would be another good legacy—interviewing Dr. King at age twelve. That could go in my obituary for sure.

"Dr. King met with Mayor Daley yesterday," my dad told me in the car. "But I guess they didn't get a whole lot accomplished."

"That's too bad," I said, pointing the air conditioning vent at my face. It was a very hot day, even into the evening. July had been sweltering so far—the temperature was above ninety degrees almost every day since the month started. At least the meeting was going to be late in the day and inside so we wouldn't get more sunburn or heatstroke.

"Dr. King doesn't think Daley understands how big a problem this issue is. Daley thinks he's doing what he can to end slums, but Dr. King says he's not doing that much at all. That's why Dr. King thinks we need more marches."

"Are we marching tonight?" I asked. I had my white sneakers on—they would be better marching shoes than my sandals.

"Not tonight, sweetie," my dad said. "Tonight we're just planning."

He pulled off the Dan Ryan and headed to Lawndale. I had never been there before. There were a bunch of large, dismal-looking apartment buildings, chain-link fences, barely any grass. "Public housing projects," my dad told me. "Such a shame what we've done to these people." I watched a bunch of colored kids frolicking around in the water from an open hydrant. They looked happy to me. Maybe they didn't realize they lived in a slum.

An ice cream truck rounded a corner. I was glad that the kids in the neighborhood could have a treat. The truck drove into a rut in the intersection of Roosevelt and Throop and seemed to get stuck. As we drove down the street, I could see the driver get out to inspect things. I could also see some kids sneak into the truck and rush out with armfuls of wrapped ice cream bars. I hoped they'd get away before they got in trouble. Slum kids were entitled to some free ice cream every once in a while.

As we pulled up to the curb on Independence, my dad said, "Oh my God."

"What, Daddy?" I asked him, worried.

"I didn't recognize the address on the flyer, but this is it. This used to be my temple."

He pointed to the stained glass Star of David above the door.

The Baptist church had been Temple Judea, he told me, the only Reform temple in Lawndale. The temple where he was in the choir, where he was bar mitzvahed. The temple the Orthodox Jews of the neighborhood frowned upon because men and women could sit together in the sanctuary.

"Did colored people go there?" I asked. Several colored men stood on the steps, dressed in suits, talking in earnest.

"Not when I was a boy," he said.

Sirens began to whine a couple of blocks away as he let me out of the car. "Maybe we should go home, Daddy," I said.

"And miss this meeting?" he said. "Not on your life."

The meeting hadn't started, but there were plenty of people milling around, most of them colored, but a few white people, too. The air inside the church was even stuffier than the outside air.

"Can you imagine your dad as a little *pisher* here?" My dad handed me a cup of punch from a card table by the door. I tried to picture him running around the building as a boy, but couldn't do it—I could just picture a miniature version of him with a big belly and a beard. Suddenly a couple of men burst into the church. More sirens flared outside.

"We need your help," one of them said. "A riot's brewing down the street."

My dad moved forward to offer his service, but the man held up his hand. "No white people," he said. "Sorry, sir. That will only make things worse."

Police had been called after the ice cream robbery. When

they got there, they turned off the fire hydrants, saying it was bad for water pressure in the neighborhood, not to mention illegal. The kids who had been playing in the water were upset and turned the hydrants back on. The police tried to turn them off again, but a bunch of people surrounded them and started yelling and pushing and throwing things and then things got crazy. People started smashing car windows and store windows. Cops started using their clubs on people left and right. I was glad the guy had told my dad not to go outside. His burnt skin looked so tender.

"We need to talk to the youth out there about civil disobedience," a woman said. "We need to tell them there's a better way to change things. They need to come hear Dr. King."

"Go get them, sister," a man said, and a group of people formed to try to talk some sense into the rioting crowd and bring them to the church. I hoped everything would calm down before we had to go back outside to our car. The church felt safe, but the world outside was dangerous, in shambles. I felt strangely responsible. If we had stopped the car to help the ice cream truck, if we had paid for all those kids to get ice cream—and my dad would have, if I had asked—maybe none of this would have happened.

People started pouring into the church, including a bunch of wound-up teenagers. A couple of them had blood on their faces. There was a lot of grumbling and fidgeting in the room. The air smelled sharp, like how gunpowder probably smells. I squeezed up against my dad on a pew and looked around to make sure no one was about to lunge at him. Dr. King finally stepped up to the pulpit. He called for an end to the chaos and said that nonviolence, not violence, was the answer to the city's problems. Just hearing his voice made me feel more calm. Then people started yelling.

"You don't know our city!" one person shouted.

"This ain't Alabama," said another.

Some other people started to chant, "End police brutality!"

The whole room filled with angry voices. I could tell Dr. King wasn't used to this kind of audience—he was used to whole stadiums falling quiet to hear him speak. Now barely anyone was listening. I watched him close his eyes and take a breath.

A man came up to the podium and said into the microphone, "Excuse me, Dr. King. Some members of the community are refusing to come inside as long as our white brothers are here. Warren Avenue Church has offered to host a separate meeting for white folks interested in the movement tonight." He looked into the crowd. All the white people except me stood up. There were maybe twenty of us there.

"Come on, Mina," my dad said, holding my hand and helping me to my feet.

"I don't want to go out there," I said, worried my heart might burst from the stress of it.

"Don't worry," he told me. "I'll keep you safe."

A big crowd had gathered outside the church, yelling and pushing toward the door. A few men escorted the white people to our cars as the crowd roared around us.

As we drove away, a group of teenage boys banged their hands on our windows and yelled things I couldn't make out.

"Go, Daddy!" I yelled as a boy snarled at me, his eyes full of hate. "Get us out of here!"

"I'm going as fast as I can, sweet pea," he said. He was trying to keep his voice steady, but I could tell he was scared, too. When we finally got out of the neighborhood, he let out a huge sigh.

"Well," he said. "That was interesting."

Interesting wasn't the first word I would have come up with.

"It's good for us to know what segregation feels like from the other side, isn't it, Mina?" he said, but I didn't think there was anything good about what I was feeling.

"It helps us understand the Negro experience," he continued, lighting a cigarette. His hand shook a little as he took a drag.

"Do we have to go to the white people's meeting, Daddy?" I asked.

"Yes," he said, and my heart sank. "Yes we do, sweetheart. We came all the way out here. If we just went home, it wouldn't mean anything." He blew smoke out the window.

Yes it would, I thought. It would mean that we were safe.

"This will separate the wheat from the chaff," my dad said. I wondered what chaff was, if it was better or worse than wheat.

We pulled up to the Warren Avenue Church. This church was smaller, with no upset throngs. Just a few white people milling around by the door. When the meeting came to order, there were only about eight pieces of wheat, or chaff as the case may be, in the room, including me. All the other white people must have gone home. Lucky them.

The man who ran the meeting said he was a Quaker. He didn't look like the guy on the Quaker Oats box, though—no black hat or white wig or rosy cheeks. This guy was skinny and pale and wore an ill-fitting button-down shirt, but he probably knew how to make good oatmeal. And he had kind, almost Lincoln-ish eyes. There was also a nun in the room. And a couple of grandmother-looking women. And a guy with a Jesus beard. And a rabbi. It was almost like a joke someone would tell about a rabbi and a nun walking into a church, although I couldn't start to guess the punch line.

I should have paid attention to the meeting, should have taken notes for an article or just so I could talk about it with my dad on the way home, but I felt too jumpy to sit still and listen. I wandered around the church, smelling candles, fingering books and statues, running my hand along the turned-off organ keys so they made funny clacking sounds, letting my heart calm down. I found a custodial closet and thought it was weird to see a mop inside a church—it seemed like God's house should be self-cleaning, somehow. I heard a few words float up from the meeting—*real estate* mostly, and *testing* and *discrimination*. A lot of numbers tossed around—rent comparisons, phone numbers, percentages of colored people in certain neighborhoods—a lot of calendar dates for potential actions. A lot of anger, but it felt different from the anger at the other church. This anger wasn't going to knock our lights out. It didn't scare me as much.

My dad was all worked up on the way home.

"That was good," he said. "I'd rather it was an integrated meeting, but it was good."

I was spent, hungry, ready to fall asleep, but my dad wouldn't stop talking. "It's so unfair, Mina," he said. "Did you know that Negroes pay more money for worse housing just because they don't have a choice?"

"Why not?" I asked, my eyes drooping.

"Because the agents won't let them see anything but slums! Because of the 'color tax'! Because of discrimination! It's abominable, Mina," my dad said. "Absolutely abominable."

I pictured the Abominable Snowman, big and white, standing in front of a nice house, our house, roaring and waving his arms, telling colored people to go away, go back to their slums. And then Rudolph the Red-Nosed Reindeer swooping in and carrying the colored people to the North Pole on his back. I guess I must have drifted off. I woke back up to my dad saying something about Thursday, mass testing, did I want to go with him?

"Mmmmm" was all I could say with my sleepy mouth, even though I wanted to ask if it was going to be dangerous, a bad part of town, a potential riot, potential heart attack.

"I knew I could count on you, Mina," he said, and patted my fedora. We stopped at a railroad crossing, and I closed my eyes again, the train chugging "I think I can, I think I can, I think I can save him" as I fell asleep.

The next morning, Tabby and I sat on the gravel by the tracks behind our house. I wanted to tell Tabby about our brush with danger, but my dad didn't want me to.

The tracks were surprisingly shiny. You would think with all that wear and tear and sun and dirt, they'd be rusty and dingy and dull, but they looked like jewelry, like a choker going across the throat of Downers Grove. Maybe that's why I liked them when I was Willie. Most people liked shiny things. Even boys.

As Willie, I adored trains—train schedules, train tracks, the works. The hobby drifted away before I was born a girl. It just wasn't lodged in my soul. I liked trains fine, but I wasn't obsessed with them the way I was when I knew every timetable of every train that came through town. I must have liked numbers better than I did in this life.

Tabby started to throw gravel across the tracks. The pieces plinked off the stones on the other side like popcorn.

I hoped no one at the lumberyard would tell us to go

away. People were funny about kids going near the tracks. Especially the third rail, which could kill you if you even touched your toe on it. Tabby wanted to run across the tracks and say hello to the German shepherd behind the chain-link fence, but I told her no way. With all her flopping around, she would touch the third rail for sure. And even if she didn't, the dog might maul her. The thought made my spine prickle.

When I was Willie, you had to hop on a train if you wanted to go anywhere. You couldn't just jump into a plane or a Greyhound bus or a car full of gas. I guess that's why I liked trains so much. They took us from Springfield to Washington, DC, after my dad became president. Trains took my dad all over the place. He wrote speeches on them. He gave speeches on them. And then, when he died, he was carried around on a funeral train for twenty whole days. I was, too. They took me out of my tomb and put me on the train with him so we could be put in the tomb in Springfield together. Guards would take the coffin—not mine, just my dad's—out of the train and open it up at every city so people could look at the dead president of the United States, but his face started changing colors and people got very upset. A few even fainted (I know I would!). An undertaker put some chalk and amber on him and then he didn't look so bad, but it still makes me feel creepy to think of thousands of people lining up to see my dead dad lying there with chalk on his face. While dead me waited in the train all alone. (Although a few times they did let children in the train to put violets and daffodils on top of my coffin. A nice touch, I have to admit.)

The ground started to shake. The tracks hummed like bugs. A train was coming.

"We better stand back," I told Tabby, who was pulling weeds out of the ground and putting them in a pile on her lap.

She reached into her pocket, took something out, and stepped toward the tracks. I could see the train coming around the bend, chugging fast in our direction.

"Tabby!" I yelled. She crouched and set whatever she was holding on the first rail. She lingered there, smiling, watching the train get bigger.

The ground got shakier. I ran up to her and tackled her to the ground before she could tip over toward the tracks and get squashed. The gravel was sharp against the side of my arm. I could tell it broke some skin in a couple of places. If I lived through the summer, I was going to end up with a lot of scars. The train swept by, roaring and sending a hot wind over us, like a dragon. I could feel Tabby quaking in my arms, but I couldn't tell if she was laughing or crying. I hoped the gravel hadn't hurt her, too.

As soon as the train was gone, Tabby wriggled out of my grip and ran to the tracks. She picked up a flat shiny thing, her face beaming. She must have been laughing.

It was a penny. With our dad's face on it. Which had been completely flattened and stretched and mangled. No amount of chalk or amber could ever make it right.

"What did you do that for?" I yelled.

"Bucky told me," she said. She put the penny in my hand. It was so hot, I wondered if it would leave a red oval on my palm.

"Well, you shouldn't do everything Bucky tells you," I said. "You could end up in a lot of trouble."

"Bucky didn't shoot me with an arrow," she said, and went running down the gravel, along the tracks. I slipped the ruined penny into my pocket and set after her.

THE LINCOLN LOG
AN HONEST ABE'S PUBLICATION

Issue 2

Mina Edelman, Editor in Chief

Tabby Edelman, Assistant Editor

Albert Edelman, Consultant

MARY LINCOLN BROKE THE BANK FURNISHING HER HOUSE, BUT YOU DON'T HAVE TO AT HONEST ABE'S!

When the Lincolns first moved into the White House, Mary's cousin said it had "deplorably shabby furnishings." Mary Lincoln would have none of that, so she went out and bought a ton of new furniture and everything else that goes in a house. She spent a lot more money than Congress gave her—a LOT more—and ended up in debt, and everyone was very upset

about this. Even Abe, who said he would never
approve the bills for "flub-dubs for this damned old
house!" (Please excuse the language, but that is
what he really said. Sometimes presidents swear. I
even read a joke Abe told that uses the F word! I
won't tell it to you, though, because some people
would get upset. I think flub-dubs and damned aren't
such bad words in comparison, so please don't send
us any complaints.)

You don't have to go into debt when you buy
furniture at Honest ABE's, but if you want to, we
have very easy credit installments! Everyone's
approved! Just be sure not to keep the bills a
secret from your husband or the rest of the country,
because if they find out, they'll call you all sorts
of names. (Coarse and vulgar and dreadful are some
of the nicer ones. So watch out!)

Willie and Tad Lincoln didn't care much for fancy
furniture. Everything in the White House was a toy
to them. So sometimes they whittled table and chair
legs into designs of their liking. I wish I could
see what they whittled there. Maybe they carved
"Willie and Tad were here" into the wood, with
little stick figures of their adventures. If you
want to carve your name into our furniture, go
ahead, but please wait until you've bought it first
and brought it home. Someone once carved "AO + FB"
onto one of our showroom tabletops--a Broyhill, if
you must know--and then we couldn't sell it to
anyone, so my dad, a.k.a. Honest ABE, chopped the
table into firewood (just like Abe liked to split
rails)! All that true love turned into red-hot

flames. And we made s'mores over it--delicious! But
don't get any ideas. We have other less expensive
ways to get firewood.

DON'T FORGET, HONEST ABE'S IS THE BEST! WOULD WE LIE TO YOU ABOUT THAT?

The next day, my dad and I marched with about a hundred people to two real estate offices in the Gage Park–Chicago Lawn part of the city. We planned to go in and ask for service, first white people, then black people, to see if there was a difference in how we were treated, in what houses were offered to us. Of course we knew there would be. We just wanted to get a record of how bad it really was. Both offices were closed, though. We were told to go to the New Friendship Church on the South Side for a mass meeting. Some of the colored guys with us stopped along the way in Marquette Park to play basketball with some white guys there, and that worked out just fine, even though it was usually an all-white park. No one got angry, but a few picnickers did look at our group with wary eyes.

Dr. King spoke at the church, and this time, people listened. This time, they only yelled because they were cheering for his words. Dr. King had good news—even though there wasn't any fair-housing legislation, the governor had made an order to ban housing discrimination. "We want that thin paper to turn into thick action," Dr. King said, and I thought of paste, dough, mud—thick things that tend to slow movement down. I don't think that's what he meant by thick action, though. He also said, "We welcome our white brothers in the movement. Together we will build a new Chicago where every child will be able to walk in dignity."

My dad smiled at me and said, "See, Mina?"

I wondered if I walked in dignity. Most of the time I was pretty clumsy.

After Dr. King spoke, a man announced that anyone who wanted to be part of the next real estate testing session should go down to the community room in the basement. I didn't even ask my dad if we could go home—I knew he would want to stay.

About half the people from the march congregated down-stairs. I looked around for Dr. King. Maybe I could interview him there—a basement felt less intimidating than a church sanctuary for a talk—but he must have left after his speech. A woman stepped up to the small podium. She was pretty, with a puffy Afro, big eyes with lots of eyeliner, and huge gold hoop earrings that just about went down to her shoulders. Her blouse was patterned bright colors, covered with a long purple vest. She wore a necklace made entirely of chunky orange beads. She made the podium look like a real one on a real stage, like the one upstairs, and not just a dinky one on the floor of a church community room. Everyone got quiet, waiting to hear her voice.

"We need to organize our testing campaign in Belmont-Cragin," she said. "We'll need both black and white families to visit real estate offices over the next two weeks."

A bunch of hands went up in the audience, including my dad's. Mine, too, as soon as I saw his.

"I'll send the sign-up sheet around," she said, and handed a clipboard down to a person in the front row.

"We also need some interracial couples to volunteer," she said. "Or we need some people to pose as interracial couples."

No one lifted a hand this time, but my dad walked to the front of the room, got down on one knee, and said, one hand on his heart, the other outstretched, "Will you marry me?"

"Daddy!" I shouted, shocked, but he didn't seem to hear me.

"Anything for the cause." The woman laughed.

The room roared. I felt my face turn hot. My dad stood up and shook her hand.

As everyone headed to the table with cookies and coffee urns, the woman came up to me and my dad.

"I guess we should meet officially," she said. "Seeing as we're going to be man and wife."

"Al Edelman," my dad said, shaking her hand again. "And this is my daughter Mina. Your future stepdaughter." He winked at me.

"Pleased to meet you," she said. "Carla Jones." When she shook my hand, her hand felt cool and smooth. Her mood ring was a swirl of green and blue.

"My dad is already married," I told her. "To my mom."

"We're not really getting married, sweetheart," she said.

"This is about something much bigger than your dad and me."

I didn't think my mom would be very happy about it. If she were to find out. She still didn't know about any of our work with the movement.

"My son, Thomas, is over there," she said, pointing to a tall teenager hovering over the tray of cookies. "I guess he'll be your stepbrother."

"Not really, though," I said. I hadn't had any sort of brother since I was Willie. I was out of practice.

"No, not really." She smiled. "Well, your dad and I better figure out our plan of action. . . ."

She slipped her arm into his and they walked over to some chairs by themselves.

I went to eat some cookies. They were butter cookies, the dry kind with a little drop of hard frosting on top. I picked up one with blue frosting and one with yellow. Thomas stood there, chewing, looking off into the distance. Maybe at nothing. There were some crumbs on his shirt. I wanted to say something to him, something about being his stepsister, but I felt too shy. I looked at him and he turned his head to me and lifted his chin a little as if to say hi and then we both looked away again.

I poured myself a cup of coffee from the metal urn. "Just to dip my cookies," I said out loud, in case anyone would be upset that a girl my age was drinking coffee. Not that anyone was paying any attention to me—everyone but Thomas was involved in animated conversation. I hated drinking coffee, but I loved the smell of it, and I loved the taste of it in other things, like ice cream or candy. The cookies soaked it up nicely, but bits fell off and sank to the bottom of the paper cup, like little sea sponges. I tried to fish them out with a red coffee stirrer, but they broke into even smaller pieces, so I tossed the cup in the metal trash can, splashing coffee onto my legs. I tried not to think about my dad and Carla planning their marriage. They leaned toward each other, eyes locked, talking and nodding and laughing.

I poured a cup of coffee for my dad and carried it over to him.

"No thanks, sweetie," he said, barely looking at me. "If I drink this now, I'll never get to sleep tonight."

"I wouldn't mind a cup," Carla said, and I reluctantly handed it to her. "I need to stay up tonight—so much to do."

"No rest for the weary," my dad said as Carla took a large gulp.

"No rest for the righteous." She winked.

"That Carla is something else," my dad said on the way home. "Did you know she works with gang members?"

How would I know that? I wanted to ask him. I don't know anything about her other than the fact that she's pretty and she likes coffee. And you asked her to marry you.

"Just today, she helped organize them to go door-to-door to call for a rent strike," he said. "And she's giving them nonviolence training. And working with the city to bring more ballparks and swimming pools to bad neighborhoods so kids can get off the streets."

"That's nice." I yawned.

"It's more than nice, Mina," my dad said, his eyes bright. "It's incredible."

When we got home, we found my mom in Roberta's room. Roberta was curled up on her bed, crying in my mom's arms.

"Where were you?" my mom shouted.

"We had another meeting—," my dad started.

"A furniture meeting that goes this late into the night?" she asked.

"Furniture manufacturers are night owls," said my dad. "They get their best work done at night."

I nodded in corroboration.

"Well, you could have called," she said. "The meeting wasn't on the South Side, was it?"

"Actually, it was," my dad said.

My mom groaned. She slipped out from under Roberta and pulled me to her. Roberta collapsed like a heap of clothes without my mom there to prop her up. "Thank God you're all right," she said. I could feel her heart beating through my cheek.

"What happened?" my dad asked.

"Eight girls were murdered on the South Side tonight," my mom said. "That's what happened."

I gasped a little and some of my mom's shirt sucked into my mouth. It tasted like her perfume.

"Nursing students," Roberta wailed.

My mom let go of me and went back to comfort Roberta.

"Do you think it's still safe for me to go to Lucy Webb Hayes, Daddy?" She pulled a pillow to her chest. "Nursing students might be a target."

"You'll be fine." My dad walked over to Roberta and patted her head. "You have nothing to worry about. At least you don't live in a slum."

"What do slums have to do with this?" My mom was livid. "These girls were killed in a town house, not a slum. A nice town house, Al. Student housing. They were tied up, beaten, stabbed, raped. Slums have nothing to do with it whatsoever."

Roberta started to wail even louder. I wanted to tell her she didn't have to worry—Robert Lincoln didn't die young. He lived a nice, long, boring life.

"I'm just saying," my dad said. "People get stabbed in slums every day. I don't see you crying over that every night."

"Where's Tabby?" I asked.

"She fell asleep watching TV," my mom said. "Before the news came on, thank God. You should carry her up to bed, Al. You're sure not doing us any good in here."

My dad breathed hard through his nose for a second. Then he saw me looking at him and winked before he walked out of the room.

"It was totally irresponsible of your father to have you out this late, especially in a bad neighborhood," my mom said, stroking Roberta's hair.

"It wasn't a bad neighborhood," I said, even though I

knew if she drove through it, she'd keep all the windows rolled up and the doors locked. She would tell us not to look at anyone because they might hit our car with a baseball bat.

"You think everyone is good, Mina, but they're not." Roberta sniffled at me, her face splotchy.

Was she right? I didn't think John Wilkes Booth was good, and I was looking for him everywhere.

"You could have been killed!" Roberta lay back, her hands over her eyes.

"Your dad should have known better," my mom said.

I wanted to say, "You two only care about yourselves! Dad cares about the world!" but I didn't think that would help anything. Especially if the subject of Dad's new fake wife came up. I just said, "I'm not dead yet," and went to my room.

I could still smell their perfume and lotion and other girl smells on my hair when my dad came in, carrying potato-sack Tabby. Tabby smelled like caramel rolled in dirt. She grunted a little when he set her on her bed but stayed asleep, even when he took off her purple suede saddle shoes and dropped them onto the floor. I felt a little jealous of Tabby then, able to sleep while we were all thinking about injustice and murder and whether people were good or bad. Her healthy heart pumping away, untroubled.

I poked my head into Roberta's room the next morning. She was busy packing her bags, carefully folding each pair of panties, each set of socks. Her room smelled like Lysol.

"So I guess you're going to go to Lucy Webb Hayes after all," I said.

"As long as there aren't any nurse killers there," she said.

"They're probably all in Chicago," I said.

"What do you want, Mina?" I didn't go in her room very often. Not that I was officially in her room—just her doorway. That was rare in itself.

"I have a medical question," I said.

She stopped folding and looked up. "Is this about your cheek?" I shook my head.

"I was just wondering," I said. "Can nurses write prescriptions?"

"I'm not a nurse yet, remember?" She picked up a pair of argyle socks. Did she own so many pairs of socks and panties she could pack them all up weeks in advance? Maybe she was just doing a practice run, trying to see how everything would fit in her set of matching blue Samsonite.

"But you will be," I said. "And I may be in need of prescriptions."

"I'm not going to help my sister become some sort of junkie."

"I have a heart condition," I told her. "And I can't seem to get any nitroglycerin."

"A heart condition?" Roberta looked at me. "Mom would have told me if you have a heart condition."

"She doesn't know," I said. "I've been having chest pains. I think it's angina—"

"Chest pains aren't something to play around with, Mina," Roberta said. "Come in here."

I squeezed through the cracked-open door. Roberta's room was neat as a pin. It looked almost as if she had moved out already.

"Can you describe these pains?" I could tell she was trying to sound grown-up. Her face was tilted in a very nurse-like way, her eyebrows scrunched down.

"They're right here," I said, holding my hands a few inches in front of my nipples. "Sometimes it's more on the left side, but both sides have been hurting. . . ."

Roberta's eyebrows unscrunched and traveled up her forehead. She tipped her head back and started to laugh.

"Angina is no laughing matter, Roberta," I said.

"Mina, you doofus," she said, laughing so hard she knocked over a pile of panties. "You don't have angina. You have tits!"

"I do not!" I crossed my arms over my chest.

"They may not look like much now, but you're getting them. Sometimes they hurt when they come in."

I should have been relieved, but this almost seemed like worse news than a heart condition.

"Don't worry," she said. I must have looked as stricken as I felt. "You're not in any danger. At least not until boys start sniffing around you."

I shuddered a little. This was something I didn't have to worry about when I was Willie. Maybe there were some advantages to dying young.

Hollister Burgeron showed up on my doorstep that afternoon holding a gun.

"You're not coming in," I said, the door still closed. I could see him through the little windows that ran up and down along the sides of the door frame. He was wearing camouflage clothes. I was glad my dad was over at Honest ABE's. I'd have to call to warn him.

"Your cheek okay?" he asked through the window.

"It needed stitches," I told him. "It got infected."

"You wanna play Vietnam?" he asked. He looked more like the good Peter Pan when he said it.

"Do you have bullets in that gun?" It was more of a rifle than a gun, I realized, with a long, thin nose, like a swordfish.

"Just air," he said. "It's not real, anyway."

"You promise not to break my skin again?"

"I'll try," he said.

"Because it hurt," I said.

"I said I'm sorry," he said.

"No you didn't."

"I'm sorry, then," he said. He probably didn't have it in him to kill my dad.

"I'll ask Tabby," I said.

Downers Grove was full of green yards—green was everywhere in the summer, but the Burgerons' lawn was crispy, scruffy. Even when the dad was at home, he didn't take care of the yard. But there were lots of green trees hanging overhead and scratchy, scraggly bushes to hide behind. A shed to hide behind, too. And the steps leading down to the cellar made a good foxhole, dank and cool and smelling deliciously of gasoline.

We decided to play Boys Against Girls. Sometimes we played Bigs Against Littles; sometimes we played Big Sister/Little Brother Against Big Brother/Little Sister. I was glad to be on Tabby's team. I hated to have to shoot her.

This time, Tabby and I were supposed to be the Vietcong. We had pressed ourselves against the back of the shed, planning out strategies in whispered gibberish—our version of Vietnamese—when Hollister and his brother, Bucky, ambushed us.

"Die, gooks, die!" they yelled, and pointed their rifles at us. Tabby and I ran screaming across the yard, Tabby throwing a grenade (really a plastic lemon juice container shaped like a lemon) over her shoulder as we tried to escape the boys.

"Oh, no you don't," Hollister said. I could feel him

gaining on me. Adrenaline rushed down my legs and panicky giggles rose up my throat as I ran willy-nilly over the crunchy grass. Hollister's footfalls shook the ground behind me; his breath came in ragged pants that hit the back of my neck. Suddenly I could feel his hand on my shoulder. Then I could feel his stomach against my back. Then I could feel my stomach hit the ground, my chin hit the ground, dirt enter my mouth. Hollister was on top of me, the nose of his rifle hard against my leg.

"I got you, you commie pinko bastard gook!" he yelled into my ear. I could smell something tomatoey on his breath, alphabet soup, maybe. I wondered if letters were smashed into his molars, what they might spell out. His hands jammed into my armpits and slid forward, his fingers stretching, curving around the front of me like they were searching for something. I squeezed my arms to my sides hard to block him.

"If you touch my tits, I'm going to kill you!" I shouted, spitting dirt off my tongue. Somehow I had enough adrenaline to throw him from my back.

"What tits?" he laughed, brushing himself off.

"Don't you touch my tits, neither, Hollister!" Tabby yelled. He always made fun of the way she said his name. *Howista.* She was sitting on top of Bucky a few feet away. He was on his stomach, not putting up a fight. She looked so casual perched on his back, like she was on a picnic blanket. Bucky was plucking the grass in front of his face, heaping it into a little pile.

Hollister lifted his rifle and pointed it at Tabby. Before I could throw my body in front of hers, he pulled the trigger. It made a little click. "Bam, you're dead," he said. She tumbled off of Bucky, screeching in high-pitched gibberish. Then he pointed it at me and killed me, too.

We were still dead when Mrs. Burgeron appeared on the back steps. She was wearing a blue terry-cloth robe. She looked like she had just woken up.

"Hollister! Bucky! What are those Edelman girls doing here?"

I wondered if I should get up from my sprawled-on-the-grass position, but Hollister put his shoe on my stomach so I wouldn't move. I pictured my intestines imprinted with his zigzag tread marks inside my body.

"We killed them, Mommy," Bucky said, running up to her. When he hugged her, the robe pulled aside. She was wearing panties underneath, but no bra. Luckily, I wasn't able to see a nipple, just the curve of one breast. It was pretty big—droopy, too. It must have hurt a lot when it grew.

"Good job," she said. She must have noticed me looking, because she pulled her robe closed tight. "Now send them home. I don't want them on our property."

When Hollister lifted his shoe off of me, my stomach rose like bread dough.

"We better go, Tabby," I said. I really wanted to tell Mrs. Burgeron I was sorry my dad made her cry. I was sorry her husband was in Vietnam. I was sorry I was looking at her chest. But she was glaring at me so hard, I didn't want to say anything.

Tabby sprang up and shook herself back to life. She let out another screechy round of fake Vietnamese and ran from the yard like a banshee. I took one last look at Hollister. He lifted his rifle at me again, but his eyes looked sad. My chest ached all the way through as I chased after Tabby.

THE LINCOLN LOG
AN HONEST ABE'S PUBLICATION

Issue 3

Mina Edelman, Editor in Chief
Tabby Edelman, Assistant Editor
Albert Edelman, Consultant

BEDS, BEDS, AND MORE BEDS!

SOME LINCOLN BED FACTS
FOR YOU. . . .

Abe Lincoln was born on a bed made of corn husks and furry bear skin.

I have already mentioned the bed that Abe died in. But did you know you can go see it for yourself, right in Chicago? It's over at the Chicago Historical Society. They bought it in 1920 from a man named Charles F. Gunther, who was a candy maker. Before he sold the bed, he kept it in his candy warehouse! Do you think it used to smell like chocolate?

The bed that Willie Lincoln (the favorite boy) died in is still in the White House. It's in the room they call the Lincoln Bedroom, even though it was really Abe's office when he was alive, not his bedroom. The bed is very fancy, with a headboard that almost goes all the way up to the ceiling. Here's what Jackie Kennedy said about it:

"When you see that great bed, it looks like a cathedral. To touch something I knew he had touched was a real link with him. The kind of peace I felt in that room was what you feel when going to church. I used to ... feel his strength. I'd sort of be talking with him."

I think she meant Abe, not Willie, when she said "him," but maybe not. Maybe Mrs. Kennedy wanted to feel a link with Willie. He was a great boy, after all!

After Willie died, his brother Tad had a goat named Nanny. Nanny disappeared when Tad and his mom were out of town, and Abe wrote a note to them that said "The day you left, Nanny was found resting herself, and chewing her little cud, on the middle of Tad's bed; but now she's gone!" So even the Lincolns had goats in their beds sometimes.

Mary Lincoln believed that Willie's spirit came to the foot of her bed at night. Spooky!

When the Lincolns lived in Springfield (the White House, too) Abe and Mary had separate bedrooms. They weren't mad at each other; it's just what people did back then if they had enough money. But sometimes Mary *was* mad at Abe, and Abe slept on a couch in his office. And sometimes she pelted him with potatoes or poured water on him through a window.

BUY YOUR BED AT HONEST ABE'S! NO ONE DIED OR GOT MAD IN THEM . . . WE GUARANTEE!

On Saturday, I put on my now-clean reporter's uniform, grabbed my notebook, and headed for the door with my dad. About a hundred people from the movement—colored and white—were going to picnic together at Marquette Park, a white neighborhood, to get the residents used to a mixed crowd, show them that colored people could live there, too. I asked my dad if we could bring Tabby—I didn't like to spend my weekends without her, and I knew how much she liked picnics—but he said she was too young to understand what we were up to.

My mom was a little suspicious. "This is an awfully long furniture convention," she said. "Especially if you're just meeting with distributors you're already working with. You can do business with them over the phone, can't you?"

"We're building community," my dad said. "Camaraderie. We're learning about each other. Seeing what we can do to make business better."

"It's really interesting," I piped up. "I'm learning a lot."

"Well, that's something." My mom smiled at me. "That's a very nice something." She was wearing a new ivory dress, fitted tight at the top with a full skirt down to the floor, big turquoise polka dots all over it, a wide turquoise belt just under her breasts. She looked very dressed up for a Saturday morning. She tipped her cigarette into the sink. If we asked her to join the picnic, she probably wouldn't want to go. She wouldn't want to get her dress all grassy.

"Just please tell me this isn't going to be on the South Side, Al," she said. "That psycho is still on the loose."

"It's on the North Side," my dad said, which I knew was a lie, but he said it so easily I was sure my mom believed him. "Plus, Mina is learning so much about the furniture world, I'm thinking I'll probably leave the store to her when I'm gone."

"I doubt that's what Mina will want to do when she grows up," my mom said. "Mina is destined for greater things than a furniture store, aren't you, Mina? My talented girl." She kissed the top of my head.

"I guess," I said. I felt a glow where her lips had been. I was too hung up on my dad talking about when he was gone to think about anything else.

"I could do great things with that furniture store, Al," my mom said, taking another puff. "I could modernize it, spruce it up, get some furniture that is more in mode."

"My customers like what I have now, Margie," my dad said. "We have a very loyal clientele. Why fix what isn't broken?"

"Because it's old and ugly and boring," my mom said, blowing a ring of smoke. "Bring in some Herman Miller. Some George Nelson. Some Knoll, for Christ's sake."

"Mina and I have to go," my dad said.

"Just be careful," she said, and wrapped me in her arms.

I had wanted to make my famous chicken-and-French-dressing sandwiches for us to take on our picnic, but there wasn't time. We stopped by The Last Word and picked up a box of fried chicken with all the sides, plus bottles of RC Cola.

The picnic was well under way by the time we got there, loads of families of all colors covering the grass. I lugged our big tartan blanket, which kept unfolding and dragging against the ground, while my dad carried the food. He said hello to lots of people as we walked by—people I recognized from different meetings and rallies—but he didn't stop until he saw Carla and Thomas sitting on their green-and-yellow bedspread. There wasn't much space near them, not even enough to open the blanket all the way, but Dad said, "Now here's the perfect spot."

"Well, hi there," Carla said with a big grin. She was eating what looked like a ham salad sandwich. She had brought real plates and cups and silverware—nothing plastic or throwaway. There was a bowl of grapes in front of her, a bowl of macaroni salad, a plate of cheese and crackers, a bowl of carrot and raisin salad, a platter of oatmeal cookies. Much more than two people could handle.

"I see you're eating like a Negro today." Carla nodded at the box of chicken.

My dad flushed. "I didn't mean anything by this," he said. "I'm not one to stereotype, Carla, I hope you know that."

"Calm yourself down." Carla smiled. "I'm kidding. I'm kidding."

Thomas was methodically picking grapes from the stem and popping them in his mouth. He barely even looked at us as I spread out the blanket as much as I could and we sat down next to them, my dad making a big *oomph* sound as he lowered himself to the ground.

"Nice day," my dad said, and he was right. The heat had broken a bit. The air was still hot, but it wasn't oppressive. The sky was a brilliant blue, full of puffy white clouds.

"Perfect day for a picnic with our integrated family." Carla winked.

I busied myself with a chicken leg and pretended not to hear. I read the motto on the napkin over and over until I could recite it with my eyes closed: "When Last Word chicken is served, a wise man never lingers. He puts aside his knife and fork and eats it with his fingers."

"How are things going so far?" my dad asked, helping himself to a breast.

"We have a few gawkers," Carla said, "but nothing troublesome. No violence."

I looked at the fringe of the picnic and saw a few white people staring at all of us movement folks filling the lawn. They looked at us like we were zoo animals, zebras whisked out of our habitat and plunked down in the middle of their neighborhood. They didn't seem to know whether to be curious or upset.

"What about Lawndale?" my dad asked. I had heard him talking to my mom that morning about more riots there. A pregnant fourteen-year-old girl was shot. Dozens of people were hurt; cops, too.

Carla's face lost some of its prettiness. "They called in over a thousand National Guards last night, did you know that? Daley blamed the movement, said we've been teaching people how to use violence."

"Shameful." My dad shook his head and lifted a sodden ear of corn to his mouth. "Nothing further from the truth."

"At least Daley and Dr. King were able to come to an agreement yesterday." Carla finished off her sandwich. "Sprayer attachments on the fire hydrants. Better access to parks and pools for the kids. A citizen's advisory committee on how police relate to the community."

"That's a good thing," my dad said, corn stuck between his teeth.

"It's not the police review board we asked for." Carla licked crumbs off her fingers. "But it's something."

The way my dad watched Carla lick her fingers made me feel funny inside. I wiped my hands on my reporter pants.

"I'm going to go play on the playground," I told my dad.

"Okay, sweetie," my dad said, looking more at Carla than at me. "Have a good time."

I sat on a swing and twisted it from side to side, digging the toes of my sneakers into the sand. I wished Tabby was there—we loved to twirl the chains of our swings together and hold hands as we spun around together until the chains separated and our hands pulled apart. We loved to push each other as high as we could and then jump off, sending sharp delicious pains up our shins when we landed. We loved to stand on the swings and pump our legs, seeing whether we could synchronize our arcs back and forth. I always hated it when we fell out of the same rhythm.

A little girl in a party dress sat down on the swing next to mine and started to flail her legs around, but it didn't make the swing move much at all. "Why are so many niggers here?" she asked me.

"They're *Negroes*, not niggers," I said. That second word in my mouth made my skin crawl. "Or you can say *colored people* if you want."

"They're only brown, and brown isn't a color."

"Yes it is," I said. "It's every crayon mixed together. Try it sometime."

She paused a second, and I knew she would try it when she got home. She would open her box of Crayolas and mash them together on a piece of manila drawing paper and see I was right. "So why are they here?" she asked.

"Because they're people just like you, and they can go wherever they want and live wherever they want," I said. My dad would be so proud that I was spreading the word of the movement. I felt like an ambassador, like I could finally walk with dignity, like the children in Dr. King's speech.

"Well, they can't live in my house," the girl said. She hopped off the swing and ran over to the slide. I hoped it would burn her legs on the way down.

When I got back to our blanket, my dad had a plate full of carrot and raisin salad and cookies and grapes. All the Last Word containers were still open but looked like they hadn't been touched in a while—the gravy on the potatoes had formed a skin, and the snips of coleslaw looked all dried out. The coating on the chicken was saggy and tired.

"Would you like some dessert?" he asked, holding up his plate.

"No thank you." Carrot salad didn't seem like dessert to me. Plus, I knew if I ate Carla's food, I would feel like some sort of traitor. I grabbed a clammy chicken wing instead.

"Some of the ladies are going to the grocery store in Gage Park to do some comparison shopping," Carla told me. "Want to join us?"

I didn't really feel like going, but then my dad said, "I'll come along, too," even though he never goes grocery shopping, and I knew I didn't have a choice.

"I told a girl over there that she should call you colored, not nigger," I said to Carla, figuring I should claim my share of glory. Thomas turned to look at me for the first time all day, his eyes wide open, like I had poked him with a stick.

Carla looked a bit startled, too, but she pulled herself together. "Thank you, Mina," she said. "That was very thoughtful of you."

My dad beamed.

"But we're trying not to use that word anymore," she told me, her voice kind but firm. "*Colored* makes it sound as if we started out white and someone colored us in."

Now my dad looked down at the remnants of the picnic, and I felt as if I had done something horribly wrong.

"Dr. King still mostly uses *Negro*," she said, "but some of us are shifting to *black* now."

I wanted to say that she wasn't really black, she was brown, but then again, I was more beige than white myself.

"It can get a little confusing," she said, "all this changing around of words. We're just trying to find ones that give us power instead of take it away."

"I'm sorry I took your power." I couldn't bring myself to look at her; a couple of tears squeezed out of my eyes and plopped onto my paper plate, sliding into the coleslaw. I couldn't look at my dad, either. I didn't want to see how much I had disappointed him.

"You didn't, Mina," she said, touching my back. "Your heart was in the right place. The movement has more power because you're in it."

I could feel my dad's hand on my back, too, could feel their fingers briefly overlap across my spine.

"Well, then," my dad said, sounding extra jolly. "Let's take that power and go shopping!"

Lots of people stared at us in the Hi-Lo Market, over a dozen proud colored—I mean black!—women, a sullen-looking teenage boy, plus me and my dad going up and down the aisles, pulling cereal and coffee and cans of green beans from the shelves, remarking over prices.

"We got a Hi-Lo in our neighborhood and we pay ten cents more for the same rice," one woman said, shaking a limp bag like a maraca.

"Now we know what the Hi-Lo is for," another woman said. "Hi prices for us, lo prices for white folks."

"It makes no sense," said Carla. "We pay more for rent. We pay more for food. And we get less money for the jobs we do."

"Makes no sense at all," my dad said, and all the colored women looked at him with their eyebrows raised, except Carla, who grinned a little and shook her head before she continued down the aisle. I saw all sorts of things I wanted—Tang, Twinkies, red licorice—but I didn't dare ask for anything. I didn't know what would make this group upset. For all I knew, Twinkies were responsible for the slums of the world. I tried to mostly look at the floor, all the wheel marks and cigarette butts smushed against the linoleum.

In the meat section, Carla said, "Well, at least they got some Parker House Sausage." She turned to me and my dad and said, "That's a black-owned product."

"I didn't see any Joe Louis Milk," one woman said. "Or Mumbo Sauce or Steward's Bleach or Rual's Diamond Sparkle. But Parker House is a start. We might not have to boycott just yet."

My dad scooped up at least five packages from the freezer. "We're never going to eat that much sausage," I told him. "Mom and Roberta are on diets, remember?"

"We're not," he said, patting his belly. "Besides," he added, "anything for the cause, right?" He smiled at Carla and she rolled her eyes but smiled back.

Between the group of us, we bought all the Parker House sausage in the store.

"You best order more of this," one woman said to the cashier.

"A lot more," my dad said, dumping his packages on the counter.

Carla gave the manager a list of products that she thought the company should stock. Especially in the black parts of town. And she told him that the store should lower their prices there, too.

"I don't do the pricing, ma'am," the manager said. He looked very scared of Carla and her band of ladies. His paper hat trembled a little.

"Then pass this along to the person that does," Carla said. "And tell him we're going to follow up."

When we came home with five packages of slightly thawed sausage, my mom said, "What in the world is this for?"

"Door prize," my dad said as he put it in the freezer.

"They're giving away *meat* at a furniture convention?" My mom had on a different outfit—a short orange dress with a band of white around the bottom.

"Cross-promotion," my dad said. "With the Amana distributor." It made me a little nervous that my dad could lie so easily. Wasn't he supposed to be Honest ABE?

"I see," my mom said, but I could tell she didn't.

"Parker House Sausage is a black-owned company, you know," my dad said.

"Why do I need to know this?" My mom looked bored.

"So you can be a more informed shopper," my dad said. "So you can help black people advance in society. So you can evolve as a human being."

"You don't think I'm evolved, is that what you're saying,

Al?" my mom asked. "You think I'm a monkey? Fine, then, I'm a monkey!" She started to run around the kitchen with her legs bent out, her fingers scratching her armpits, making hooting sounds. Her dress rose up, and I could see her salmon-colored underpants. I wanted to laugh, but I wasn't sure she was trying to be funny. I sort of felt like crying, too. My dad didn't seem to know what to do, either. He stood there looking helpless for a moment, but then their eyes caught and both of them started laughing and my dad said, "Come here, you monkey," and scooped her up in his arms.

The next day, Richard Speck was arrested for killing those student nurses. There had been one other student nurse in that town house who had hidden under a bed and had been able to avoid the attacks. She recognized his "Born to Raise Hell" tattoo when he was brought into the hospital after he tried to kill himself.

It's weird that Richard Speck knew that he was born to be bad. I wonder if he knew he was bad in the life before this one. If he was John Wilkes Booth, I could certainly breathe a sigh of relief because he had been arrested. Although I would breathe a deeper sigh if he had gone ahead and really killed himself, because even if he was born into another baby's body when I was twelve, he probably wouldn't be dangerous again until I was a grown-up. I had a feeling he wasn't John Wilkes Booth, though. He would have gone after our family instead of a house full of women. Unless he was just practicing before he got to us.

Roberta was very relieved. So was my mom. And since my dad and I were about to embark on more "furniture conventions," it was good that she was less worried about a crazy guy running around loose.

The real estate testing started the day after that. My dad and I dressed up nice—no reporter uniform this time, which was probably for the best, since I never got around to interviewing anyone, anyway. I wore a dress, which I didn't do that often, and my underpants felt very open to the world. My mom gave me an extra long hug before we left.

"You look beautiful," she said. "I know you'll wow those furniture guys."

"We'll see," I said.

"Get some great material for the newsletter," she said, and I felt a wave of guilt. "I bet you'll win the Pulitzer prize!"

We drove to the Parker and Finney real estate office on West Fullerton, in the Belmont-Cragin area. The people inside seemed glad to see a white man and his white daughter come through the door. A few couples had already tested Parker and Finney, and the office hadn't passed, to say the least.

"Can I help you, sir?" a woman asked. She was wearing a suit jacket and skirt that seemed to be made out of some sort of nubby carpeting. It looked way too hot for a summer day, although the office was filled with whirring fans. Her hair was sprayed into a helmet.

"Yes, thank you," my father said, taking on his store showroom voice, his showman voice. "We're looking for a house in the area. What do you recommend?"

"I'll need some more information, sir," the woman said. "How many bedrooms, for instance? How many baths?"

"We'll need at least three bedrooms," my dad said. "One for my wife and myself, and one each for our daughter and son. Perhaps an extra for guests. A good neighborhood, of course," he added. "No crime."

"Of course, sir. Only the best and safest for our clientele."

She pulled out binders full of information about different homes in the area. Brownstones and red-brick duplexes and aluminum-sided ranch houses. I looked at each photo, and I thought, "I could live there. And there. And there." But when I tried to picture our family in each place, all I could imagine was me and Tabby running through the empty rooms.

"This one looks good," my dad said, pointing to a house made of tan-colored stone. It was kind of fancy, with scrolled metal columns supporting the awning over the front door and a big brass doorknocker shaped like a lion's face.

"Would you like to arrange a walk-through?" the woman said.

"I'd love to—," he started. Then Carla and Thomas walked in the front door of the office and he leaped out of his chair and my heart started pounding. We hadn't really rehearsed this—we had just talked vaguely about what we were going to do. I hoped we'd be able to pull it off.

"Honey!" my dad ran to Carla and gave her a huge hug. She looked a bit startled by his embrace at first, then wrapped her arms tentatively around him. He held on to her for what was probably a bit too long, then gave Thomas a clap on the back.

"I'd like you to meet the rest of my family." My dad guided them over to the woman, who clutched her stomach like she had just eaten some bad fish.

"Carla, Thomas, I'd like you to meet— Sorry, I don't think I ever got your name."

"Mrs. Richard Kelly," the woman stammered. She didn't hold out her hand.

I couldn't understand why women called themselves by their husbands' names like that. Your own name, your own self, shouldn't disappear after you get married. Although I suppose her own name could have been Richard. Or maybe it was something else but she was too flustered by black people to remember it and she said a man's name by mistake.

"So, about that house." My dad sat back down. There were only two chairs on our side of the desk. I stood up so Carla could sit next to my dad. I thought it would be weird if she and Thomas were both standing behind us, like they were at the back of a bus. Thomas didn't look at me when I stood beside him.

"I'm sorry, sir," said Mrs. Richard Kelly, rearranging things on her desk. "I just remembered that house is in escrow. It's not available."

"What about that brownstone, then?" he said. "That looked like a sweetheart of a deal."

"Off the market, I'm afraid," she said.

"That cute little brick number, with the rose garden?"

"Unavailable."

"Is there anything you can show us today?"

"I'm afraid not, sir." Her voice was steady, but she looked at him with hate in her eyes. She knew he had duped her.

My dad had kept calm until this moment, but now he stood up and banged his hands on her desk, making her jump. "This is an outrage!" he said. "This is sheer and blatant discrimination! Your office is going to be hearing from us again, you mark my word. Us and hundreds of others like us!"

Mrs. Richard Kelly looked as if she was about to have a heart attack. "If you don't leave right now, sir," she said, "I'm going to have to call the police."

My dad was about to start in with another harangue, but Carla touched his arm and nodded curtly to Mrs. Richard Kelly. "Thank you for your time, ma'am," she said. "This has been most enlightening."

Mrs. Richard Kelly opened and closed her mouth a few times but didn't say a word.

I noticed there was a dish of bridge mix on her desk. I didn't really like the dark-chocolate-covered nuts and dried fruit—they were a treat only grown-ups could enjoy—but I grabbed a handful anyway and stuck out my tongue before I followed my fake family, seething and triumphant, out the door.

"That was great!" my dad shouted out on the sidewalk. "I feel so alive!"

"It's not great," said Carla, guiding us down the street. "It's horrible. It's horrible they won't let me even look at a house because of the color of my skin. It's horrible that my son and I can't make a home anywhere we choose."

"You're right," my dad said, sobering up. "It is horrible. Criminal." Then he started grinning again. "But we make a great team, the four of us, don't we?"

"I'll give you that." Carla smiled back at him. "No more banging on desks, though, Al. We're promoting nonviolence here, remember?"

We stopped for milkshakes and French fries at a diner around the corner. The hostess seemed startled to see white and black people together. She tried to tell us all the tables were reserved in the half-empty restaurant, but after my dad complained, she put us in a booth in the back corner. All the other people eating there stared at us as we sat down. Carla gave them a big sugary smile; my dad glared at them. I wasn't sure what to do, so I just ignored them. I dumped the bridge mix in the center of the table. It left dark smears on my palm. I tried to rub them off with a napkin, but the chocolate was too sticky, and little shreds of napkin stuck to my skin. I excused myself to go wash my hands. By the time I got back, my dad and Carla had polished off all the bridge mix and Thomas was standing by himself by the jukebox. A bunch of people looked at him as if they thought he was going to pick up that jukebox and hurl it at them or race at them with a pocket knife, but he ignored them like I did.

Simon and Garfunkel came on through the speakers. *Hello, darkness, my old friend.* I wouldn't have guessed that's what Thomas would choose, but "The Sound of Silence" made sense for him in a way (because he was so quiet, not because of the darkness part—that would be discrimination if I thought that).

"I like my apartment," Carla was saying to my dad as I slid into the booth, "and I don't want to move—there's too much organizing to do in my neighborhood for me to up and leave. But if I wanted to move to another part of town—or the suburbs, God forbid—man, I'd have a rough go of it."

"You know who else had a hard time finding a house in Chicago?" I asked.

"Do tell," my dad said as the waitress plunked a steaming pile of French fries in the middle of the table and left without saying a word to us.

"Mary Lincoln," I said.

"Mina is quite the Lincoln aficionado," my dad told Carla as he shook ketchup onto the side of the plate. "She writes a newsletter for my store."

"*The Lincoln Log*," I said, making Carla laugh. "And I did a report at school." I was glad my parents had never seen my notes from my teacher. I don't know why I had felt compelled to tell Mrs. Turner about my past life—I hadn't told anyone else. I was probably so excited to have just figured it out for myself, I couldn't hold it inside. It was a good thing she hadn't spilled the beans.

"My store has a bit of a Lincoln theme," my dad said, and I felt proud that it was my idea.

"Brother Abraham." Carla nodded with appreciation and swiped a fry through some ketchup. Thomas sat down next to her.

"Anyway," I said, "Mary Lincoln moved to a fancy hotel in Chicago after Abraham Lincoln was shot, but she didn't have much money, so she had to move to a cheap boarding-house in Hyde Park. She told everyone her name was Mrs. Clarke so they wouldn't know that the Lincolns were so poor. And then she couldn't afford that, so she had to sell her clothes!"

"Mary Lincoln on the South Side," said Carla. "I had no idea."

"How'd she get so poor?" Thomas said. His voice startled me. Sometimes I forgot he knew how to talk.

"She spent too much money," I said.

"Sounds familiar." My dad looked at me and rolled his eyes in a dramatic way. Usually I would join him in joking about my mom, but it didn't feel right to do that in front of Carla.

"And the government didn't give her much to live on," I said.

"Too bad," Carla said, "after all her husband did for our country."

He's sitting right across the table from you, I wanted to say. But the way she looked at him made me think that she might have known that already.

Rain started to pour as we walked Carla and Thomas to their car. My dad took off his suit jacket and held it up like a canopy for all of us to huddle under. Thomas stayed out in the rain, but Carla and I bent under my dad's arms and let him shield us as we ran down the street, just like a real family.

When we got home, my mom was out. Roberta was supposed to be looking after Tabby, but she had shut herself in her room and let Tabby run around the house willy-nilly, barely dodging the cleaning lady. It made me sad to think of Tabby playing by herself while I was out in the world doing important work. Before I could catch up with her, the doorbell rang. I could see Hollister through the narrow windows next to the door. He didn't appear to have any weapons on him. He was dripping wet from the rain. His head looked smaller with all his hair plastered to it. His Windbreaker stuck to his body like plastic wrap.

I opened the door. "You better wipe your feet if you're coming inside," I said. "And don't sit on anything until I put a towel down." My mom was very protective of her furniture.

"I'm not coming inside," he said. I was kind of relieved. "I just wanted to tell you that my dad got his arm blown off today. He's coming home next week. So you can tell your dad that my dad's not coming home in a body bag after all!"

Hollister looked right into my eyes for a moment, his eyes hurt and proud all at once. I wondered if some of the wet on his face was from tears, not rain. I wanted to say something to make him feel better, but I didn't know what. Instead, I blurted out, "Is his arm coming home in a bag?" Hollister's face scrunched up like a fist. He turned and ran away.

Tabby stepped up near me holding Fido, the cat's body draped down the front of her dress. Stretched out like that, Fido looked almost as long as Tabby. I scratched his furry white belly. I circled one of his cat arms with my hand. With the fur pushed down under my palm, his arm felt thin as a twig. I had never noticed how thin Fido's limbs were. It would be way too easy to break them. I wondered what blew Hollister's dad's arm up. A gun? A grenade? TNT? Was his arm rotting somewhere on the jungle floor? Were bugs and birds nibbling it away? Were his fingernails dirty? Was his palm facing up or down? I shuddered and let go of Fido.

"Hollister's dad lost his arm," I said to Tabby.

"Maybe he left it on the car," Tabby said. Our mom had a tendency to leave her purse on top of the car. Whenever a car pulled up next to ours with a person frantically gesturing to the roof, it didn't take us long to figure out why.

"Ha ha," I said. "That's not funny, Tabby."

"I hope he finds it," she said, and walked away, swinging the cat in front of her like the pendulum in a grandfather clock. Fido was a very patient cat. I felt funny that I couldn't tell Tabby about our day at the real estate office. I could still smell Carla's sweet hair oil from when we crouched under my dad's jacket together. I wondered if Tabby could smell it on me, too, if it seemed weird to her, since she knew my normal smell.

I heard Tabby talking to Bucky on the phone a little bit later. I hoped she wouldn't say anything stupid, but she did a much better job than me. "I'm sorry about your dad's arm," she said, and I wished I could rewind time and say the same thing to Hollister. I asked her to ask Bucky to put Hollister on the phone, but Bucky told Tabby to say that Hollister didn't want to talk to me, and his mom didn't want him to talk to me, either. I touched my cheek. The cut had healed, but it was going to leave a small scar. Nothing like an arm blown off, of course. But something I would remember the rest of my life, however long that might be.

The rain broke, and Tabby asked if I wanted to go play in the mud. I didn't really feel like getting dirty, but I told her I would after I changed out of my dress. When I came back downstairs in some scruffy play clothes, my dad was firing the cleaning lady.

"I don't want to oppress you anymore," he said. "It's so typical—the rich white people oppressing the poor black woman."

"We're not rich, Daddy," I said, but I don't think he heard me. If we were rich, I'd be able to buy the battery-powered kid-sized Jeep I'd been drooling over in the Spiegel catalog. If we were rich, we'd have a pony in our backyard. If we were rich, my mom wouldn't always be so worried about money.

"Are you firing me, Mr. Edelman?" The cleaning lady sat on the kitchen chair as if someone had just kicked her in the stomach.

"I'm emancipating you," he said. "You're free! Go to school! Become a doctor, a teacher! Open your own business!" He waved his arms up and down so much, I think he almost levitated right off the linoleum.

"I got rent to pay, Mr. Edelman," she pleaded. "Bills. I got a sick husband. I need this job."

"You need a job that doesn't subjugate you." My dad was

fervent. "You don't need to do our dirty work. We can clean up after ourselves."

I looked at her hands, white cracks on brown skin. Knuckles big as grapes. She cleaned my toilet. She wiped my old toothpaste out of the sink. She stripped my dirty sheets, she carried my trash out of my room. She knew all the parts of me I left behind—crumpled drawings, snotty tissues, the crusty stuff inside my underpants. I knew nothing about her.

"Mr. Edelman . . . ," she started, but my dad touched her elbow and helped her to her feet. She shrugged on her brown cardigan—it was way too hot for a cardigan but she wrapped it around herself like it was twenty degrees outside. Some of her curls, white and black, sprung out at the back of her neck, like figs I once saw growing right out of the trunk of the tree.

"We did a good thing," my dad said after he shut the door behind her. I watched her walk toward the bus stop, head bent forward, a Marshall Fields bag full of cleaning supplies slung over her arm. I didn't know where that bus took her. When she wasn't in our house, I forgot about her. I forgot about her even when she *was* in our house. "We did a very good thing," he said again, his eyes ablaze.

So why did it feel like we were committing a crime?

My mom screamed bloody murder when she got home. "What do you mean you fired the cleaning lady?" With her high heels on, she was taller than my dad. I thought she was going to bend over and devour him like a praying mantis.

"You don't expect me to scrub toilets, do you? You don't expect me to clean my own grout?"

"You're fully capable, Margie," my dad said. "You have two hands. Fine working arms."

"And a manicure. And a busy social calendar. And no desire to touch our family's filth!"

As if on cue, Tabby ran into the kitchen, her dress caked with mud. My mother sighed in exasperation, her head tossed back. She stormed out of the room before Tabby asked us if we wanted to visit her dirt diner.

"I have dirt burgers," she said. *Dirt* sounded like *dut*. *Burgers* sounded like *boogas*. "And dirt soup and dirt mashed potatoes."

"I'd like a slice of mud pie," said my dad, obviously still very pleased with himself.

"You'll be eating crow, Albert Edelman!" my mom yelled from upstairs. "That's what you'll be eating, mister!"

I watched clots of mud tumble from Tabby's dress to the floor the cleaning lady had swept and mopped that very morning. I wondered if any of us would ever pick it up. Maybe none of us would. Maybe the dirt would keep accumulating until we were all wading through mud, like pigs. Oh, how the mighty Lincolns had fallen.

I walked upstairs and said through my mom's closed door, "It's not so bad, really. At least we're still alive."

"Just leave me alone, Mina." She groaned. I could hear her head smack against the pillow. Or maybe it was the pillow smacking against the wall.

I wanted to say, "You wouldn't say that if you knew I'd be dead within the year," but I decided against it.

"And tell your stupid idiot father that he's not welcome in this room until he hires someone to clean it up," she said.

When we were the Lincolns, we had one particular special maid named Elizabeth Keckley, who we called Lizabeth or Lizzie. She wrote a book, *Behind the Scenes, Or, Thirty Years a Slave, and Four Years in the White House.* There's a whole chapter in it called "Willie Lincoln's Death-bed."

Lizzie wasn't actually there when I died—she was "worn out with watching" me waste away while my parents had their fancy dinner party downstairs—so I don't know what happened exactly when my soul flew off. But she was called for and helped wash me and dress me, and she was there when my dad lifted the sheet from my face and saw me dead for the first time.

Lizzie said, "I shall never forget those solemn moments—genius and greatness weeping over love's idol lost. There is a grandeur as well as a simplicity about the picture that will never fade. With me it is immortal—I really believe that I shall carry it with me across the dark, mysterious river of death."

I wonder if she did. I wonder if the cleaning lady my dad fired was really Lizzie and she did remember that moment of my dad crying for me. That could be why she was so upset when my dad fired her. How could he do such a thing to her after she's remembered him for over a hundred years?

Tabby and I went to the furniture store the next morning. It was a slow day—not many customers. I could understand why. I wouldn't want to buy heavy furniture on a hot summer day, either—it would be like buying a winter coat when you want to wear a bathing suit. But my dad did have a small section of patio furniture for sale, too—glass tables with iron legs that would look good topped with a big pitcher of lemonade.

"When's the next issue of the *Log* going to be ready?" Phyllis asked.

"I'm not sure," I said, and she must have been too busy with her filing to hear because she said, "Great! Can't wait!"

I was having trouble coming up with more Lincoln furniture facts. I did find one new reference to a chair when I scoured my library books, but it disturbed me too much to write it down—it was about Tad dying. He had picked up a nasty bug when he and my mom went to Europe, and he got even more sick after they got back to their hotel room in Chicago. Water was filling his lungs. If he didn't sit upright, he would drown, and that seems like one of the worst ways to die, I think, drowning in your own body. Our mom bought a special chair to hold him up and strapped him to it, but then one day he turned blue and slumped over in the chair and he was dead.

I looked over at Tabby opening and closing the leg part of a recliner and wanted her to be able to live forever. At least if she got pleurisy now, a doctor could give her antibiotics and she would probably be fine.

My dad hung up the phone and told Tabby to find a place to hide for hide-and-seek. She rushed across the showroom; I could hear her giggle as she shimmied under a bed. I was about to go find a hiding place, too, but my dad pulled me aside.

"Bad news, Mina," he said in a low whisper, and I was worried that he knew something about my health that I didn't. "Two real estate offices are trying to stop Governor Kerner's ban on housing discrimination."

That wasn't good news, but I was relieved that it wasn't anything about me or our family.

"And those offices are near here," he said. He explained that the town of Weston, which wasn't too far from us, was in the running to get a huge atomic accelerator built there. Five states wanted it, especially our Land of Lincoln, but then the NAACP said it shouldn't be in Weston because of all the unfair housing practices. That's why the governor asked for no discrimination in housing, so Weston could still maybe get the accelerator and all the jobs and money that came with it. But real estate agents didn't like that and said they should be able to discriminate if they wanted to. It was all a big mess.

"You know the Argonne labs," my dad said, and I nodded. The labs were just down the road. Both of Hollister Burgeron's parents worked there—his mom as a secretary, his dad as a technician—at least he used to before he went off to war. I wondered if he'd be able to work there now with just one arm. "Only two percent of the black workers there have been able to find local housing." He wasn't whispering anymore. "It's a travesty."

"You can't find me!" Tabby yelled.

"I better go hide, too," I told my dad, worried that my sister would have breathing troubles if she stayed smushed under the bed for too long.

"We can't keep hiding from the truth," my dad said. He watched as I climbed into a wardrobe. I closed the door just as he yelled, "Ready or not, here I come!"

"Where is that Tabby?" he said in a funny voice. "Where could she be?"

I could hear him open drawers and move chairs and pretend to have a hard time finding her. I could hear her squeal and giggle and scream as he pulled her out from under the bed, could hear him chasing after her, both of them breathless.

"Why don't you help me find your sister?" he asked her, and I could feel my heart start to pound in the darkness, even though I wanted them to find me.

On Thursday night, there was a mass meeting at the New Friendship Baptist Church, but my dad went by himself. He said it was going to go too late into the night for him to bring me, and the neighborhood was still kind of unstable.

"Then you shouldn't go, either!" I pleaded with him. He needed me to be his bodyguard. I hated the thought of him there alone, with people maybe banging on his car window, maybe hating him for being a white man at a mostly black meeting.

"We'll do more testing on Saturday, sweetheart," he said. "And we're having another picnic then, too."

"Be very, very careful," I told him, and he promised me he would before he grabbed his briefcase and raced out the door.

I was glad to have the evening with Tabby—we arm wrestled and played Trouble and drew funny pictures of Roberta and made up a song about cheese—but in the back of my mind, I kept thinking about my dad. I tried to stay awake to make sure he got back in one piece, but I conked out at some point. I remember waking briefly to the smell of Carla's hair oil and thinking it was weird that Carla was at my house in the middle of the night, but then I felt my dad's scratchy beard against my cheek and fell back to sleep, happy he was home and safe.

Sixty-one black people and forty-seven white, including me and my dad, went back to the Belmont-Cragin part of Chicago on Saturday to test thirteen real estate offices. The first one we went to was supernice to me and my dad and showed us a bunch of pictures, but then told us they had to shut down the office as soon as Carla and Thomas walked through the door. At the second one we went to, the agent seemed a little distracted as he showed me and my dad some nice pictures of houses—his office had probably gotten a lot of traffic that day, and he maybe didn't know what to make of it. I really liked a photo that looked like a fairy-tale house; the agent called it "Tudor style." I could picture me and Tabby running through that house very easily. After Carla and Thomas joined us, with all the hugging and introducing that involved, the agent seemed a lot more distracted. He pulled out a different book and said, "I think you'd be more at home here," and showed us pictures from Carla's own neighborhood.

"No, we'd be more at home in that Tudor one," I said, and the agent shook his head and said, "It's just not possible," before he asked us to leave.

When we met up with the other testers at Riis Park, we found out that only one real estate agent offered all of his regular listings to black people. One out of thirteen places, one person out of over a hundred who tried. Carla had been to the Chicago Freedom Movement Assembly earlier that morning and learned that movement people had already documented 121 cases of housing discrimination in Gage Park. She said that 150 rental units were open there, but none of them were offered to black people. There was a picnic happening that day in Gage Park, too. I took notes about all of this in my notebook so I could write an article about it later. I loved my blue spiral notebook—it was like my brain outside my body, a place where I could put all my thoughts.

My dad had told me to bring my bathing suit because there was a pool at Riis. I wore mine under my dress because I didn't like to change in front of people. A bunch of other kids, grown-ups, too, brought theirs as well—Carla and Thomas included. When we showed up at the pool, though, we were told it had been closed for the day.

"There's glass at the bottom of the pool," a guy in a park district uniform told us, a little sneer on his face. The pool was calm and blue and inviting behind the chain link. The chlorine smelled delicious.

"Can't you clean it up?" someone asked.

"It's a hot day," my dad said. "A weekend. Shouldn't our children be able to get some relief?"

"You want relief?" the guy said. "The bathrooms are right over there."

My dad looked like he wanted to punch him.

"How long could it take to clean up some glass?" Carla asked, trying to keep her voice reasonable.

"Longer than you'll be here," the guy said.

"I hope you know that Mayor Daley agreed to allow equal access to city parks and pools," Carla said. "Enforced by the park district and police. You should at least have gotten a memo."

"This isn't about equal access, ma'am," the guy said. "This is about broken, jagged, foot-piercing dangerous glass at the bottom of the pool." He made each word sound more and more menacing, like someone telling a scary story.

"Right," my dad said.

"And now if you'll excuse me." The guy turned on his

heel and walked back to his office. A lot of people booed at him, but at least no one tried to hurt anyone. We found out later that at Gage Park a bunch of white people had jeered at the black picnickers and started throwing things at them; one person got hit by a rock.

My dad hadn't brought any food along this time. He knew Carla would pack enough for all of us, and she had—roast beef sandwiches, potato and ambrosia salads, big wedges of honeydew, peanut butter cookies.

"My fake wife sure knows how to feed me right," he said, and it made me feel a little sad for my mom, with her cans of Metrecal slimming drinks, her bottles of Tab, her sad little pieces of skinless chicken.

We had a break from movement stuff for a few days. My dad had to catch up with paperwork at the store, and I was glad to have some time with Tabby. We rode our bikes around Downers Grove and saw Hollister Burgeron and his family coming out of the five-and-dime. Hollister's dad's arm was just a stump hanging from his short-sleeved dress shirt, wrapped in bandages with a brownish stain at the bottom. His eyes looked spaced out, like he didn't really know where he was. Hollister's mom saw me and Tabby and made their whole family turn the corner just to get away from us. Hollister swiveled his head to look at me before they disappeared from view. I thought about telling Tabby we should follow them and spy on them, but I didn't want to see any more of that seeping bandage.

Hollister showed up at my front door later that day.

"So you saw it," he said through the window.

"Yep," I said.

"It hurts him a lot," he said.

"I'm sorry," I said.

"More than an arrow." He looked defiant.

"And that hurt a lot," I said.

"He cries at night," he said.

"I'm sorry," I said. It made me feel funny to think of a grown father crying, especially a big-shouldered man like Mr. Burgeron.

"He might get a fake arm," he said. "With pinchers at the end. Or a hook."

"That's good," I said. "Do you want to come in?" It felt funny to talk to him through glass, like he was an exhibit at a museum. Or I was. Or like one of us was visiting the other in jail.

"Maybe tomorrow," he said.

"Hey," I said, "don't you think that black people who work with your parents should live here?"

"At your house?"

"In Downers Grove," I said, but I suddenly pictured my whole house filled with black people. My mom would have a fit, even though she said she didn't have any bones that discriminate at all.

"Downers Grove is white," he said.

"It doesn't have to be," I said.

"You're weird," he said. "I'll come in your house tomorrow." And then he was gone.

If Hollister Burgeron came to my house the next day, it was after my dad and I left for Chicago. My dad had cooked up a huge pan of Parker House sausages for breakfast—I was getting sick of sausages at this point—and announced that he was taking me to the city overnight. The furniture manufacturers were having a little party, and they were so happy with the work we were doing, he said, they were going to put us up in a hotel for the night.

"Al, you've been promising me a weekend in the city for ages," my mom said. She was eating a grapefruit half sprinkled with saccharin. No sausages for her.

"We'll go soon, my sweet," he promised. "You probably wouldn't like these accommodations, anyway—we're staying at the Travelodge, not the Palmer House."

My mom wrinkled her nose.

I wondered if the Palmer House was related in any way to Parker House sausages. I guessed not, even though they were only two letters different.

In the car that afternoon, I asked my dad where the party was going to be held.

"You silly goose!" He ruffled my hair. "There's no party!"

I felt something sink inside. Of course there was no party. My dad was getting so good at telling stories, even I had believed him.

"What about the Travelodge?" I asked, bracing myself.

"No Travelodge, either." My dad smiled, and all my

visions of individually wrapped hotel soaps and wonderfully scratchy hotel sheets dissolved into mist. "We're having an all-night vigil."

"All night?"

"In front of a real estate office in Gage Park. It will be so powerful, Mina! We're going to show them we're serious about this. We're going to show them we're willing to pray on our knees all night for equal access."

"On our knees?" This was getting worse and worse.

"I know you're not used to praying, Mina," my dad said. "But I have a feeling you'll pray better than anyone there." Maybe he was right. I was probably still a "peculiarly religious child," like I was when I was Willie. I tried to steel myself for the challenge. I would try to prove him right. I'd be the best pray-er the world had ever seen. Maybe it would make up for not being able to break the "sanitized for your protection" seal on top of a Travelodge toilet.

Only five people—four black, one white—were at Halvorsen's Real Estate Office when we arrived—some of them on their knees, some just crouching down, all of them looking at the ground as if the sidewalk were talking to them, or maybe it was a mirror that they couldn't stop looking into. Some of them were moving their lips but weren't making any sounds out loud. That was praying, I supposed. A couple of people looked up when we arrived, a bit nervously, as if they worried we were going to knock them over, but when they saw it was us, they smiled and looked back down. I could tell my dad was disappointed that Carla and Thomas weren't there yet.

"Guess we better settle in, Mina," my dad said. "We're here for the long haul."

He grunted a bit as he lowered himself to his knees. I lowered myself, too, glad I was wearing my khaki pants and not a dress. I could feel every line and bump of the sidewalk through the fabric—it would be even worse with bare skin. The heat of the pavement glowed all the way to my bones.

I kneeled there for what felt like forever, sometimes putting my bottom down on my legs, sometimes bringing it back up again. I whispered to my dad to find out how long we had been there, sure it was over an hour already, but it had only been fifteen minutes. This praying was harder than I had anticipated. I had to keep changing positions, standing up sometimes, sitting Indian-style sometimes, wiggling my legs sometimes, but always trying to look down, so it would seem like I never stopped praying. I could tell my dad was uncomfortable, too—he would make little groans and sighs, and sometimes I could hear his joints pop and crack. More and more people knelt down with us as the day progressed. It got a little easier to kneel with time. I tried to tell myself I was a rhinoceros, like the one that I saw the last time we went to Lincoln Park Zoo. A rhinoceros wouldn't be able to feel the sidewalk through its tough, heavy hide.

"I have to pee," I whispered to my dad.

"I wouldn't mind finding a bathroom, myself," he said. Both of us creaked and grunted as we stood up and shook our legs. We tried a nearby diner and a watch repair shop and a pharmacy and a shoe store, but none of them would let us use their restrooms. They probably saw us at the vigil, my dad said. He must have been right, because when we tried a bathroom at the gas station around the corner, they let us in right away. My dad bought two Hershey's bars with almonds from the little snack counter there.

"Isn't that cheating?" I asked my dad.

"This isn't a hunger strike, Mina," my dad said. "We need the energy." Still, he made us eat them before we rounded the corner again.

When we got back to the real estate office, a lot more people were there, kneeling and crouching and praying, including a bunch of college-age-looking kids, and Carla and Thomas. I was surprised at how powerful the sight was. When I was in the middle of it, I didn't really have a sense of how the vigil looked from the outside. Now a crowd of gawkers had formed around the kneelers; we had to break through them to find our spots on the ground.

"Glad you could make it," Carla whispered, smiling, as we settled back down.

"We were here earlier," my dad whispered back. "We just had to make a pit stop."

"I went before I came," said Carla. "I doubt anyplace around here would let me use their facilities."

"Try the gas station around the corner," my dad said.

"They might let your white *tuchis* in," Carla said, "but my Negro *tuchis* could be problematic."

"Not for me." My dad grinned.

Someone shushed him, and his face turned red. I don't think he realized that he had stopped whispering. I wondered how Carla knew a Yiddish word like *tuchis*.

My knees were smarting. I thought it would be easier to kneel after getting used to it before, but if anything, it was harder. My knees were raw from the earlier kneeling, and now I could really feel the sidewalk bite into all the sore places. I tried to keep telling myself "rhinoceros knees, rhinoceros knees," but that didn't seem to help much. I kept shifting my weight, shifting my position, but my body felt achy and tired and I found myself even hungrier than before the candy bar. I could hear some other stomachs grumbling around me, could hear whispered conversations about dinner. I could also hear a lot of praying to God, to Jesus, to Mayor Daley, to Dr. King, to the real estate agents, to all people who needed to change, to all people and beings who could possibly help. I wished I knew how to pray right. My dad was wrong—I wasn't the best pray-er there. But I would try to learn.

"Daddy," I prayed in my heart, "let your Abeness shine through. Do what you can to make this a better place for everyone to live. You've done it before. You can do it again."

I looked over at him and he smiled at me as if he heard my prayer and would do whatever he could to make it come true.

As the vigil grew, so did the group of onlookers. They were as quiet as we were at first, just watching. But over time, they started to taunt, and some started to yell. Some even started to lunge forward, pretending they were going to jump on us. Maybe they just wanted to see us flinch, hear us gasp. If so, it worked. I asked my dad if we should leave and he said no, that giving in to bullies is always wrong. We need to show them we're stronger than that. I didn't know if I was stronger, though. My legs felt brittle and bruised, and I was so hungry, I thought I might pass out. I couldn't imagine staying there all night. I thought I might have to curl up in a ball on the sidewalk and sleep, but then I wouldn't be able to protect my dad, especially if he fell asleep, too.

The crowd got louder and louder and more and more threatening. Finally at ten, a preacher stood up and told us we had done our work. We had made a difference. We could all go home. "Get some rest," he said, "so you can join us for the march to Gage Park tomorrow."

The group stood with a lot of groaning and cracking and sighing and hugging. Some people, including Carla and Thomas, planned to go over to a church for a meeting. I could tell my dad wanted to stay, but I convinced him to bring me home.

"Maybe we should stay at the Travelodge," he said. "Your mother's going to wonder why we didn't stay overnight at the Travellodge."

"Tell her I had a stomachache and wanted to be in my own bed," I said. I didn't care about little hotel room towels anymore. My stomach *did* hurt from emptiness. My whole body hurt from kneeling, or attempting to, for almost eight hours. I fell asleep immediately in the car; I don't even remember my dad carrying me up to my room.

Both of us slept late on Saturday, so we missed the march on Gage Park, which was a good thing. My dad talked to Carla on the phone and found out that residents had thrown bottles at the marchers. She said the police promised more protection for the Sunday march, which was a relief.

All I wanted to do was stay in the tub and soak out all the stiffness from the night before. Hollister Burgeron came over, but I wasn't ready to get out of the tub yet, so I told my mom to tell him to come back later. He never did. But Tabby came into the bathroom and stripped off her clothes and climbed right into the bubbles with me.

Tabby and I had taken baths together ever since she graduated from the kitchen sink. I loved to feel our slippery limbs slide against each other under the bubbles. We would lie back, head to foot, in the water, my leg bumping her arm, her leg sliding against my arm, our hair slithering between each other's toes, both of us rubbery as dolphins. Steam filled the room and settled in my lungs, heavy and warm. But now that my chest was hurting, I felt a little funny in the tub with her. I wanted to hide each inch of my body under a tall wall of foam. Especially after Tabby found some hairs I didn't know I had.

"Mina," she said, pressing her chin to her chest as she floated on her back, her belly rising over the water like a pale island. "Why do you have hairs on your angina?"

"I don't have angina after all." I sat up, pulling more bubbles toward my chest. "I thought I told you that."

"Yes, you do," she said. "Here." She touched me between my legs underwater with her big toe. It made a tickle go all the way up to the top of my head.

"Vagina," I said. "And I don't have hair—" But then some

127

bubbles drifted away, and I could see what she was talking about. A few dark, straight hairs marring what used to be a smooth mound of skin. Some of them lifted from my body and waved around underwater like little sea worms. I wanted to yank them out, but I didn't want to do it in front of Tabby.

"You're turning into a gorilla," she said. I loved how *gorilla* sounded in her mouth—*gawihwa*.

"I guess so," I said.

I knew Tabby's body so well—her scar, the dimples by her knees, the way her bellybutton was a circle while mine was an oval, the way her right ear came up in a little point like an elf, the way her head smelled when she got sweaty, the way her littlest toes barely had nails. I probably knew her body better than my own. And now mine was changing into something neither of us knew.

I asked my dad if Tabby could go to the march with us on Sunday. I wanted to spend as much time with her as I could before we didn't recognize each other anymore.

"I don't know," my dad said. "Tabby can be very disruptive."

"But isn't that what we're trying to do?" I tried to fill my voice with passion like the people in the movement. "Disrupt things? Things can't change unless we disrupt them, right?" I knew some of the lingo would persuade him.

"That's very true, Mina," my dad said. "That's very true indeed."

"So . . . ?" I said.

"So, why not?" he said, tugging on his beard. "Why don't we invite Tabby along?"

When my dad and I were in the car alone together, I always felt very grown-up. We were off on our grown-up mission, and a seriousness hung in the air, even when we joked around with each other. With Tabby in the car, the air felt more festive and squirrely.

"We're going to a parade?" she asked, bouncing in the back seat.

"It's sort of like a parade," I said.

"A parade of justice!" My dad raised one fist up in the air. His cigarette nearly burned a hole in the fabric on the ceiling.

"I think you should drive with both hands, Daddy," I told him, and he put his hand back on the wheel. I turned my head so smoke wouldn't get in my face.

"You can't tell Mommy about this parade, though, okay?" my dad said. "Or Roberta."

"Okay." Tabby slid across the back seat from one side to another. "Can we ride on a float?"

"I don't think there will be any floats," I said.

"Can I do a baton?" She scrambled her hand around as if she were doing tricks.

"That's probably not a good idea," I said. Someone could take the baton and hit her with it. I had heard about people getting hit with the sticks from their own signs. At the meetings, they always said that if you want to bring a sign, bring one you can hold in your two hands.

"Sounds like a stupid parade to me," Tabby said, and slipped down to the floor of the car as if she had no bones. Maybe it wasn't the greatest idea to bring her after all.

"This parade will make all other parades look stupid, Tabby," my dad said, lifting his arm again. "This parade is the smartest parade ever! This parade makes things happen in the world. The Saint Patrick's Day parade doesn't do that, does it? The Saint Patrick's Day parade doesn't change the world one bit."

"But they dye the river green and that changes the world," Tabby said. We went into Chicago for the Saint Patrick's Day parade once. My mom's stepmom was on one of the floats, wearing a traditional Irish costume. We waved and waved from the curb on Michigan Avenue, but she didn't see us, or if she did, she didn't wave back.

"That's different," my dad said. "Dyeing the Chicago River green doesn't improve anyone's life. And it may even hurt the fish." He took a big drag off his cigarette and tossed it out the window.

I learned in school that engineers reversed the flow of the Chicago River in 1900. They were worried about pollution from the river getting into Lake Michigan, where all the city's drinking water came from, so they turned the river around and made it flow away from the lake instead of into the lake. If people could figure out how to do that, it seemed to me that they should know how to make other things change, too. Giving black people good houses seemed like it should be a much easier task than turning a whole river around.

We parked the car near the small lagoon at Marquette Park. The grass was already full of people. A man with a crew cut and a white T-shirt came up to us as soon as we closed the car doors.

"Are you with the march or against it?" he asked.

"With it, of course," my dad said. "How could anyone be against this march?"

"Goddamn nigger lover." The man scowled and spit at my dad's feet. A big glob of it just missed him; it perched in the grass like a huge cartoon dewdrop.

"Maybe we should go home, Daddy," I said, grabbing his arm as the man stormed off to find his next spitting victim.

"Sweetheart," he said, "this gives us all the more reason to be here."

The plan was to march through the park, then down Kedzie Avenue and end up at Halvorsen's Real Estate Office for a prayer vigil. A steady stream of people moved down the grass like it was a conveyor belt, their straw hats bobbing as they walked. We stepped into the stream. Tabby made her mouth sound like a kazoo, circus music buzzing her lips.

"When are we getting to the parade?" she asked.

"This is it, peach pit," my dad said. He nodded and waved to some people we had seen at other marches and meetings. They nodded and waved back and lifted their signs in return—A PREJUDICED CHILD IS A CRIPPLED CHILD; END SLUMS; HOW LONG?

"Only one person is wearing a costume," she said, pointing to a short woman in black and white.

"That's a nun, Tabby!" I said.

"No it's not," said Tabby. "It's a penguin."

The nun *was* waddling a bit like a penguin, side to side. She probably had a bad hip.

"That's not very respectful, now," my dad said, but he was Jewish, so how could he know what would bother a nun?

"Maybe it's a peng-nun," Tabby said, and my dad tried not to laugh.

"A lot of people of faith have joined the movement, Tabby," my dad said. "Not just nuns. Priests, rabbis . . . "

Tabby sighed as if that was the most boring thing she had heard in her life.

Then a green bottle whizzed in front of our chests. It slammed straight into the arm of the nun. She tumbled to the ground in a heap.

All the marchers gasped at once—a loud sound together, like a monster inhaling. But there was some cheering, too. "We got one!" someone yelled from the edge of the grass. And then, as people bent down to help the nun to her feet, rocks started to fly. A couple of men fell to the ground, blood on their heads.

"Daddy!" I screamed. He scooped me up with one arm and Tabby with the other and ran forward through the crowd. I tried to put one arm around his head to protect it, but he told me he couldn't see with my arm up there.

"Barbarians," my dad grunted, out of breath. "What are they thinking?"

I looked through the rush of frantic marchers at the people lining our path, jeering and tossing things at us. There was a girl, probably my age or a little younger, winding her arm back to throw a rock. There was a woman who yelled, "Burn them like Jews!" which I could tell rubbed my dad the wrong way. A bunch of teenage boys with crew cuts ran together, holding a long rope with a noose at the end of it, singing the Oscar Mayer Wiener tune. Instead of wanting to be an Oscar Mayer Wiener, though, they sang that they wanted to be Alabama Troopers so they could hang niggers legally.

"I'm going to have to put you down, girls," my dad said. I could feel his sweat seeping through the side of my shirt as he set me on the ground. "Keep holding on to me."

We wrapped our arms around him and staggered forward. It felt as awkward as a three-legged race but a lot less fun. At least for me. When I looked across my dad's stomach, I could see Tabby's face all lit up.

"I thought we were supposed to have police protection today," my dad said. He still sounded breathless. His face was pink and dripping with sweat.

I had seen police cars in the parking lot by the lagoon and a few officers with clubs along the edges of the grass, but hadn't noticed any since the rocks started flying. Another one came screaming past. It hit a nearby woman on her hip. When she fell, other people tripped on her and fell, too.

"Daddy, watch out for your head!" I yelled. I squeezed his waist even harder.

The marchers careened off in different directions. I could feel the grass beneath my feet turn to gravel and then asphalt. It was hard to see where we were exactly, so many people were rushing around us. Then I heard glass crash and saw that a rock had gone through a store window. Then another. Then another. I heard yelling and saw a couple of people, including a cop, with bloody faces from the shattered glass.

"White Power! White Power! White Power!" young men chanted as they lifted bottles in the air.

"Polish Power!" one old man chimed in.

"People Power!" my dad yelled back. "People Power! People Power!"

I wanted to tell him to be quiet, to not bring attention to himself, but then other people around us started chanting the same thing, and pretty soon everyone was shouting it so the throwers wouldn't have known who to target. I started to say it, too, and it made me feel a little bit less scared to hear my voice with other voices. It felt like our voices made a bubble around us, something that could keep us safe. But then another bottle came hurtling through and almost hit me in the leg, and I got scared all over again.

By the time we got to the real estate office, there was such a screaming mob, the organizers decided we wouldn't be able to hold our vigil in peace. They told us to meet at a nearby church instead.

A man who sounded a little like Dr. King stepped up to the pulpit. Dr. King was in Atlanta at his own church that day. The man started to talk about the importance of being peaceful in the face of violence, but it was hard to pay attention to him. Tabby was squirming around so much and then Carla and Thomas slipped into the pew next to us.

"Such madness out there," my dad whispered to Carla. "Are you okay?"

"I think I twisted my ankle." She grimaced and lifted her foot. It looked a little puffy over her green sandal.

"You should elevate that," my dad said. Carla scooched sideways on the pew and put her foot up on the book holder built into the back of the pew in front of us. It didn't look like a very comfortable position; the edge of the book holder was so narrow, I was sure her foot would slip off. I guess my dad must have thought the same thing. He gently lifted her foot and put it on his knee instead. That still looked awkward, but I guess it was more comfortable, because both she and my dad were smiling, even though they weren't looking at each other.

When it was time to walk back to our cars, I was scared to step outside. I was sure people would be waiting outside the church, bottles and bricks and rocks in hand.

"Maybe we should call a cab and have it drive us to our car," I told my dad.

He just squeezed me and said there was safety in numbers. Carla asked if we could give her and Thomas a ride home; it was a short walk, but she wasn't sure she could handle it with her ankle all swollen. Of course my dad said yes. He even put an arm around her so it would be easier for her to limp across the grass. Tabby ran ahead of us, spinning and jumping, stopping every once in a while to pick up something from the ground. She found a small sign that someone had dropped and hefted it proudly above her head. From behind her, I couldn't see what it said. A few people hung out on the outskirts of the grass, jeering at the marchers, but when they saw Tabby, they whooped and lifted their hands in the air. She loved the attention, and danced around even more. When she spun toward us, I could finally see the sign. It had a big swastika right in the middle of it.

"Tabby!" my dad yelled. "Put that down right now!"

"Why?" she asked, shimmying around.

My dad let go of Carla's waist, stomped over to Tabby, and yanked the sign out of her hands. He tore the sign in half and dumped it in a trash can.

"Do you even know what that is?" he asked.

"It's a star," she said, defiant.

"It is not a star," he said. "It's a swastika. It's for Nazis. Hitler."

"White Power!" some of the people yelled. I looked at their hands. No rocks that I could see.

"The Jews had to wear stars," my dad said.

"I want to wear a star, Daddy," she said.

My dad sighed. "We'll talk about this later," he said. I hadn't seen his face so upset in a long time. He stormed on ahead, lost in thought. Tabby and I ran to catch up, leaving Carla limping a few steps behind us, holding on to her son's arm.

The weeping willows around us started to look scary in the dusk, like the trees in *The Wizard of Oz*, ones that would come to life and grab you. Or throw fruit or rocks at your head.

"Look at all that smoke." Carla pointed to dark columns rising in the distance. "I wonder what's going on."

"Firecrackers!" said Tabby. Her voice was excited, but her face still looked glum from Dad taking away her sign.

"I doubt that, honey." My dad turned to us. His face still looked troubled, too.

When we got closer, we saw the truth—a bunch of cars in the parking lot had been set on fire. Flames were roaring from the metal.

"Where's our car?" I asked, frantic.

"In that lot somewhere," my dad said. He picked up his pace. Thomas and Carla struggled to keep up with us.

I started to cry. I hated to think of my notebook, the seat I sat in, our tissue box, our radio, burned into crisps.

"It will be okay, Mina," Carla said.

"You don't know that!" I said. Tabby grabbed on to my hand.

"It's just a car," she said, hobbling toward me. "We're all in one piece."

"For now!" I yelled. Who did Carla think she was?

"I don't see our car," my dad said as we got close to the parking lot. Fire trucks and police cars swarmed the place. It was hard to tell what kinds of cars were burning, but he was right—none of the bumpers or frames looked like ours. A couple of cars were unburned but on their sides. Neither of those were ours, either.

Thomas, who barely ever talked, said, "Could that be it?"

His voice was so deep, it startled me. I followed his finger pointing to the lagoon. And there, bobbing in the dark water, was our familiar beige roof.

"Sonofabitch!" my dad yelled.

Tabby giggled. "Daddy sweared," she whispered to me.

"What the hell did they do that for?" He looked like he was ready to punch someone.

"How are we going to get home, Daddy?" I asked, but he didn't answer.

"We'll find a way," said Carla. "Don't worry, Mina." But I didn't want her to comfort me, even if she was my fake mom.

"We'll march!" Tabby started marching around in circles, making her circus kazoo mouth.

"I don't think we should be so close to the flames," I said. "What if a car blows up?"

"I think we're a safe distance," said Carla. She was shifting around, trying to find a comfortable way to stand on her busted ankle.

"I'm going to go talk to the cops," my dad said. "You all wait here."

Tabby kept marching around in circles. Thomas leaned against a tree. Weeping willow strands hung in front of him like tentacles. Carla sat down on the grass and sighed. I wanted to follow my dad, to protect him from the flames, from any leftover pyromaniacs, but I knew he didn't want me to. I watched him get smaller and smaller, the flames rising.

"I bet they'll be able to tow the car out of the water," Carla said. "Air it out, it'll be good as new."

I just took a deep breath and thought of my notebook, all the ink floating off the paper into the murky water. Even if I aired the book out, the pages would be warped, the words gone.

My dad came back a few minutes later, looking about as tired as I'd ever seen him.

"The police will give us a ride to the station," he told me. "We can either call your mom from there, or we can take a cab home."

"Do you think they'd give us all a ride to my place instead?" Carla asked. "She probably doesn't want to get a call from a police station at this hour."

She probably doesn't want to get a call from some strange woman's apartment at this hour, either, I thought.

"That's a good idea," my dad said. "A husband should be able to see his wife's apartment, after all."

He and Carla looked at each other for a good long time. It made me nervous. I glanced at Tabby to see if she could see it, too, but she was oblivious, holding on to a weeping willow strand and twirling as if it were her dance partner. Thomas still stood under the tree, looking bored.

"You're only a fake husband," I said to my dad. He and Carla looked at me as if they had both woken up from a nap and didn't know where they were. I think I could see my dad blush, even under his beard, even in the dark.

We piled into a cop car. I sat on my dad's lap, Tabby sat on Carla's lap, and Thomas sat by himself in the middle of us. It was weird to be in a criminal's seat. I hoped no criminal germs would creep through my dad's clothes and into mine. I didn't want to catch any badness by mistake. Tabby wrapped her fingers around the cage separating us from the cops and bounced around on Carla's lap. Carla looked like she was trying to be patient, but every once in a while, she cringed when Tabby kicked her in the ankle or came down on her lap too hard. The car smelled like sweat and leather. A boy-car smell. The air was full of smoke from the cop's cigarettes.

We only had to drive a few blocks, into a part of Chicago I hadn't seen before. The buildings looked run-down, the grass patchy and sparse in front of them. Trash on the sidewalk. Lots of men and teenage boys hanging around outside, watching the cop car. I wondered if they thought we were criminals behind the windows. Maybe they would be afraid of us when we got out, or maybe it would make them want to jump us all the more. I imagined this was one of the neighborhoods my mom had warned my dad about.

"Here we go," said Carla, and the car eased to the curb.

"White man like you best watch out around here," the cop told my dad as he let us out, and a shiver went all the way through me.

"It's not that bad," Thomas said, looking down at the sidewalk. His voice was like a bass drum—I could feel it in my chest bone.

"You know, sir"—my dad straightened himself up after bending out of the car—"you should have been the ones watching out for us at that march. We were told we were going to have police protection, and what happens? Nuns get hit by rocks. Cars get set on fire. And, need I remind you, sir, white people were the ones doing the damage? I feel much safer in this neighborhood, to tell you the honest truth."

"I don't want any trouble, sir." The cop scrunched his eyebrows and put his hand on his holster. I must have gasped out loud, because Carla put her arm around me and said, "Shhh."

"Thank you for the ride, officer," she told the cop. "I'm sure the next march will be much more peaceful." He nodded and got back in the car.

A couple of the men on the corner started to sing "We Shall Overcome" as the cop car drove away. Carla smiled at the men before she ushered us to her front door. Her building looked like it might have been kind of fancy at some point—it was red brick, four stories tall, with turret-shaped windows jutting out of the top floor—but paint was peeling around the doors and windows, and a couple of scribbles of graffiti I wasn't sure how to read marred the wall. The concrete walkway had a bunch of chunks taken out of it. The entryway inside smelled like pee.

But Carla's apartment—one of the ones with turret windows—was nice, even though I was out of breath after walking up four flights of stairs. The furniture was old, but not in a bad way. Not dirty or torn. You could just tell a lot of people had sat on it and slept on it and put their glasses and plates on it. If my dad offered Carla a whole new house of furniture, I had a feeling she would tell him no. Plants were on nearly every surface, even the windowsills. Chicago

Freedom Movement signs were everywhere, too, stacked up against the wall, leaning next to chairs, piled on top of the dining room table, along with flyers and clipboards and notebooks and folders and newspapers. In neat stacks, not strewn all over the place.

Thomas slunk off to his room without a word. Tabby tried to follow him, but he closed the door in her face.

"Don't mind him," Carla said. "Thomas is just upset because Bob Dylan crashed his motorcycle a couple of days ago. It's nothing personal."

Tabby didn't seem to care. She shuffled her feet on the shag carpet as she walked back over to me and then touched my arm to give me a shock. I could see the blue spark shoot from her finger, hear it crackle between us.

"Let me get you something to drink," Carla said, but my dad said, "You sit down. You need to get off that ankle." She smiled and sank onto the couch. I watched my dad watch her slip off her sandals and set her foot on the coffee table, on top of a *Freedom Now* newsletter, before he retreated to the kitchen.

"We have some lemonade, fresh squeezed, in the icebox," Carla called to him. "And some cookies in the pantry."

"Cookies!" Tabby yelled, pinching the end off an aloe vera plant and touching the inside, slick and moist, to my arm, right where the shock had been.

"First things first," my dad said. He came out of the kitchen with a dishrag full of ice and set it on Carla's foot. His hand stayed there awhile, adjusting the rag so it wouldn't slide off and spill all over everything.

"What a good husband you are," she said. When she noticed me staring at her, she added, "A good fake husband."

"Anything for my fake wife." He winked and went off to get our snack.

I was curious to see what kind of cookies black people kept in their kitchens. Maybe you could buy whole other brands of cookies in black neighborhoods. I was kind of disappointed when my dad came back with a box of vanilla wafers. What could be more white than that? The lemonade was delicious, though. Tangy and full of lemon pulp—or "pup," as Tabby called it. Which made me picture tiny translucent dogs, sea monkeys with floppy ears.

My dad and Carla talked for a while about movement stuff, all the usual subjects, plus the angry mob, the lack of police protection, the fact that our car was under several feet of murky water. I tried not to eavesdrop too much while I followed Tabby around the living room and watched her peer into every potted plant, stroking the leaves, pulling off shreds, burying her face in fronds. I tried not to notice the way my dad and Carla sat right up next to each other on the couch, the sides of their arms and legs touching, the cushions beneath them bowing together.

"It's getting late," Carla finally said. "Shouldn't you be calling your wife?"

"You're right," he said, even though he didn't seem eager to get off that couch. He looked at her for another moment before he slapped his hands on his thighs, stood up, and walked to the phone. Carla wobbled on the couch a bit as he rose, her cushion slanting back to normal. She grabbed an ice cube from the bundle on her ankle and, sighing, touched it to her lips.

"Margie!" my dad yelled, too brightly, into the phone. "How are you, sweetheart?"

I could hear my mom's voice coming through the ear holes of the phone, tinny and loud, but I couldn't make out the words.

"No need to worry, honey," my dad said. He sounded like a man in a commercial. A fake husband talking to his real wife. He rolled his eyes a bit and smiled at Carla. "The girls are fine."

More tinny noise from my mom.

"Where are we? Well, that's a bit of a story, Margie. And the story ends with a little car trouble. Which leads me to this—do you think you could come get us?"

Tabby yelled, "Hi, Mommy!" at the top of her lungs and waved as if my mom could see her over the phone. One of her pigtails had come undone; she looked half wild, bits of plant stuck in her hair.

"We're near Ashland, not too far from Marquette Park," my dad said.

The buzz of my mom's voice grew more shrill. "No, I am not crazy for bringing the girls here! This is a fine community." He nodded at Carla. She leaned back on the couch and closed her eyes, her mouth pressed shut.

My dad's face clouded. "Well, we'll just take a cab then," he said. "No need to get upset, Margie." He turned his back so we couldn't see him anymore and lowered his voice. Carla crossed her arms over her chest. I could tell she was straining to hear his end of the conversation. He was good at whispering. I could only make out "love you" before he hung up.

"Not too many cabs come out here this late," Carla said.

My dad nodded. He looked a bit rattled.

"The phone book's under that fern," Carla said. "Try Leon's Taxi—they're local. They'll likely be glad for a long-distance fare."

"What are you going to tell Mom?" I asked in the cab. My dad and I usually got our stories straight in the car on the way home. We would decide who was at the furniture meetings, what food they served, what their secretaries were wearing. How it was going to affect business. All lies, of course, which I knew was wrong, but I loved helping him come up with stories, being co-conspirators.

"I think we're going to have to tell her the truth this time," my dad said from the front seat. He had told the driver he sat up there because he didn't want to make the driver feel subservient, like a chauffeur. He wanted to let him know that they were equals. "Our car could show up in the papers, on the news."

If my mom found out where we had been, she probably wouldn't let us go to marches or meetings anymore. It was all my fault. I never should have suggested Tabby come with us. If she hadn't come, maybe our car wouldn't have ended up underwater. Maybe a nun wouldn't have been hit with a rock. Maybe the march would have been perfectly peaceful. Then I looked over at Tabby, sound asleep, her cheek pressed against the window, her pointy lip pulled up above her teeth, and I felt guilty for thinking anything bad about her. Telephone wires dipped and rose outside like lines of dreams coming out of her head.

I must have drifted off, too, because the next thing I knew, we were in our driveway.

"Nice place," the cabdriver said. He sounded tired.

"I'm doing my damnedest to make it possible for you to get a place like this if you want one," my dad said.

"I don't think $14.35 is going to buy me a house like this," the driver said. "Much as I appreciate the fare."

"I'm talking about the movement, sir, not the fare. Speaking of which"—my dad's head wobbled as he dug around in his pockets—"I'm going to have to get some cash from my wife."

My mom appeared in the driveway in her white satin nightgown and robe, her hair in curlers, her feet bare. She looked very angry. My dad rolled down the window. "Margie, do you have a few dollars?" he asked.

My mom snorted. "Oh, yes. I always keep cash in my peignoir."

"I'll just be a minute," my dad told the driver before he left to get the money. My mom opened the back door and, wrinkling her nose at the sweat smell of the cab, scooped Tabby off the seat. The driver craned his head to look down the front of my mom's nightgown as she hoisted sleeping Tabby into her arms, but she didn't seem to notice. She didn't seem to notice he was there at all.

"Come on, Mina," my mom said, but I decided I'd better

stay in the cab until my dad got back so the driver didn't think we were trying to stiff him. She glared at my dad as they crossed paths on the front steps.

My dad paid through the window with a handful of coins and a bunch of crumpled bills.

"That should cover it, plus a little extra," he said as he let me out. "I wanted to give more of a tip, but I wasn't expecting to need a cab tonight, and I didn't have the cash on hand. . . ."

The driver sighed and said, "I need to head back to the city."

"We're going to make life so much better for you, sir," my dad said.

The taxi peeled out of our driveway, sending little bits of gravel against my legs.

I wanted to stay up so I could help my dad explain what we had been doing, but both of my parents told me to go to bed. I pressed my ear to the floor of my room so I could hear them talk downstairs, but I barely needed to do that. Their shouting came through loud and clear. I heard my mom yell, "What in God's name were you thinking?" I heard my dad yell, "This is important, Margie! I want the girls to be part of it! I want them to grow up knowing they've made the world a better place!" It went back and forth, back and forth, my mom saying we could have been killed, my dad saying he wouldn't let anything happen to us, my mom saying Negro housing wasn't our responsibility, my dad saying yes, it was, it was every decent human being's responsibility, my mom saying he should get off his high horse, my dad saying she should try to ride one every once in a while.

I was too rested from my nap in the cab, too worried about what was going to happen next, to fall asleep. I went downstairs around one in the morning to get a snack and heard my dad talking. His voice sounded soft and gentle and I was glad that he and my mom had made up and were talking like civilized people again. When I reached the kitchen, though, I saw he was on the phone. The only light in the room came from its dial.

"I better go," he said as soon as he noticed me and hurriedly put the phone on its cradle, turning the whole room dark.

"Who were you talking to?" I asked, fumbling over to the wall.

"Santa Claus," he said. "I was just filling him in on your goodness."

"Very funny." I turned on the light, making him wince, and opened the pantry door.

"Actually, I was talking to President Johnson. I had some ideas to share with him."

"Ha ha." I grabbed a box of Ritz.

"What? You think your father isn't important enough to talk to the president of the United States in the middle of the night?"

"Who were you really talking to?" I asked, pulling out a sleeve of crackers.

He took a deep breath. "Carla," he said. "I just wanted to let her know how everything went."

"You called her this late?" I asked.

"We're both night owls," he said, and for some reason, I thought of Nauga, the crazy-looking pillow creature that the Naugahyde representative sent to my dad's store. It looked kind of like a bat or an owl with pointy ears and a wicked sharp-toothed smile. A yellow starburst, kind of like a saw blade, radiated out around its eyes. The letter that came with it said, "Sadder but wiser mothers pray for permanent furniture. The Nauga answers those prayers. With the hide off its back. Naugahyde vinyl fabric. Naugahyde is so tough, it breaks a kid's spirit." I didn't want to play with it after reading that. I made my dad hide it in a dresser whenever I came to the store. Tabby wanted to bring it home, but I refused. Why would we bring a spirit-breaking toy into our house? My dad ended up giving it to the Burgerons. I was kind of relieved when I went over there one day and found the Nauga ripped open on the floor of Hollister's room, stuffing tumbling out.

"I guess we're not going to see Carla again," I said as I tore the end off the cracker sleeve.

"Why would you say that?" my dad asked, grabbing a stack of crackers before I had a chance to take one. He sounded stricken.

"Because Mom said we can't go to marches anymore."

"Your mother is not the queen of the universe," he said, crumbs tumbling onto his beard. "As much as she would like to believe she is."

"So I can still go with you?" I nibbled around the edge of the Ritz. I liked making it into a smaller and smaller circle.

"Not right away," my dad said, "and not all the time. We're going to have to be a bit sneaky about it."

"Like you calling Carla at one in the morning," I said, and my dad choked on his mouthful of crackers.

"Like me taking you when your mom is somewhere else." He took a long sip of water. "And we can say we went to the library. Or on a hike. She doesn't have to know."

"I don't think we should take Tabby anymore," I said, even though it stabbed my heart to say it. My circle of cracker was almost gone.

"That's probably for the best," my dad said. "And I shouldn't take you all the time, either."

I felt a different kind of stab this time.

"It's not that I don't love to go with you, Mina," my dad said, "but these marches can get dangerous. Your mom's right about that. There shouldn't be violence around the movement, but there is, and I don't want you to get hurt."

I'm not the one you should be worrying about, I wanted to tell him.

"I'm sure we can still do real estate testing together, Mina," he said. "And some meetings. And marches north of the Loop. But nothing that could potentially explode."

I thought of Hollister Burgeron's dad, his arm blown off. Abe's skull bursting during a play. The Nauga splayed open on the floor. Anything could explode, even things that seemed impossible to break.

PART TWO

A house divided against itself cannot stand.

—ABRAHAM LINCOLN

My mom wanted all of us to pitch in more, now that we didn't have a cleaning lady. Roberta and Tabby were upset, but I didn't mind. Washing the dishes gave me time to think.

I put the scalloped potatoes pan in the sink and was letting the faucet tease the last shreds out of the corners, when my dad walked into the kitchen.

"I've been thinking, Mina." He settled down into an orange molded chair and lit a cigarette. "I've been thinking that if we can't go to the marches, we should bring the marches to us."

I poured soap into the pan, watched foam billow up over the edges.

"It's the *Chicago* Freedom Movement, Daddy," I said. "Not the Downers Grove Freedom Movement." I couldn't imagine a bunch of black people with signs marching down Main Street. The people of Downers Grove would have a heart attack.

"It should be the Everywhere Freedom Movement, Mina," my dad said. "Just because we don't have slums here doesn't mean that everything is hunky-dory."

I dumped the lamb bones into the garbage can, rinsed the bloody smears they left on the plate.

"In fact," my dad said, "it may even be worse here. We have, what, two black families in town?"

There was one black boy a grade below me at Avery Coonley. He always ate lunch by himself. I didn't see him at recess very often; maybe he spent it in the library.

"I'll bet if we tested the real estate offices here, every last one of them would fail," he said.

It would be different doing real estate testing in our own town. We couldn't do it with Carla and Thomas here, since everyone knew who my dad was. Who we all were. We weren't nearly as famous as when we were the Lincolns, but my dad's ads did put us in the public eye. Plus his shop was right downtown. And Downers Grove wasn't even technically a town; it was so small, it was actually a village. So if my dad showed up at a real estate office and then Carla walked in and he introduced her as his wife, the real estate agent would look at my dad and say "What sort of cocka-mamie stunt are you trying to pull here, Al?"

"I'm going to give Carla a call," he said. "Maybe she and Thomas could visit, do some testing, the two of them."

"She doesn't have a car," I said. I rinsed the lamb blood off the plates, put them in the dishwasher.

"The train comes right here," my dad said. "I could pick them up at the station."

"Wouldn't it be weird if someone saw you drive her to the real estate office?"

"She could use my car," he said. "I'll walk home from work."

"Your car is still in the shop."

"Your mom's car, then."

Mom would really love that. "What if Carla doesn't know how to drive?"

"Carla knows how to drive," my dad said, grinding his cigarette into the blue metal ashtray. "Carla can do everything a white woman can do. More, even!"

"I think maybe you better talk to Mom about this first." I dumped the last of Tabby's "dinner soup" down the sink, chunks of lamb fat and potato inside her glass of milk.

"Your mother will come around, Mina," my dad said, but he sounded like he didn't believe his own words.

"You better talk to her," I said again, and he closed his eyes and leaned his head back like he was going to sleep. I put my hand on my belly and felt all the food roil and churn under my shirt.

My parents hadn't been talking a whole lot lately. My dad slept on the couch in the den most nights. They barely looked at each other at the dinner table, and when they did talk, their voices sounded hard and flat. My dad's voice sounded different, warmer, whenever he talked to Carla on the phone. He laughed more. He got excited about things. Kind of like when he talked to me.

"Do you believe in reincarnation, Daddy?" I asked when he sat down on the foot of my bed that night. Tabby snored softly a few feet away. My heart pounded a little. I was worried he would think I was crazy. My stomach still ached from too much food, but nothing bad had happened—I hadn't thrown up or anything.

He squeezed his beard. When he let go, it sprung out wide, like a flower opening in one of those speeded-up movies.

"I don't know, sweetheart," he said, in a voice just a little above a whisper, to not wake Tabby. "Perhaps I do in a way. I know my father did."

"I do." I sat up and curled my legs into my chest.

"Well, that's an argument for reincarnation right there," he said.

"How's that?" I asked.

"You could be my father reincarnated."

I shook my head. "I don't think so," I said.

"Why not?"

"That would be too weird," I said, "being your dad and your kid at the same time." Plus, I know who I used to be.

"I think it would be lovely," he said. "I could start calling you Pops. You could start telling me how to play stickball."

"All you do is hit a ball with a stick." I shrugged.

"That's exactly what he said!" My dad slapped his knee, making the whole bed bounce. "See? You're my father, Mina!"

I didn't like this turn of the conversation. What if he was right?

"His name lives in you, you know," my dad said.

"My name isn't Weissman," I said. I always thought that

Weissman was a funny first name. It was more like a last name. Weissman Edelman. At least his middle name didn't have something with "man" in it, like Weissman Herman Edelman. Although I think it was something like Schlomo, which was probably even worse.

"Your name starts with *W*," my dad said. "That's Jewish tradition, giving the first letter of the first name of someone you love who died. That means their soul lives in you. So my father's soul lives in you. Hence, you're my father." He looked kind of sad as he tweaked my nose. He probably wouldn't have tweaked his father's nose, so I doubt he really believed it. Besides, *W* was also for William.

"I don't think most people know that Jews believe in reincarnation," my dad said. "I don't think most *Jews* know that Jews believe in reincarnation."

"I didn't know," I said. "But I'm not really Jewish."

"My father had a book about Judaism and reincarnation," my dad said. "I'll see if I can find it for you in the attic."

As he walked out my door, he turned his head and said, "You can be Jewish if you want, Mina. You can believe anything you want to believe, no matter what anyone says. Even Dr. King."

I wondered what Dr. King would have to say about reincarnation.

"I don't believe I'm your father, Daddy," I said, and it made him look a little sad. He tossed me a kiss anyway before he reached for the chain in the hallway ceiling that pulled down the attic door. I held my breath, worried the ladder would slide out too fast and hit him in the head, but it came out in its usual slow unfolding way, bringing the cedar and spiderweb smell of the attic with it. My dad climbed up the rungs and disappeared through the hole in the ceiling. I tried to stay awake until he came back down, but he was up there a long time.

The next morning, I found an old book on the foot of my bed—*The Reincarnated Jew*. It was covered with dull blue cloth, the words stamped on front in white. It made the whole room smell like sharp, sweet dust. Tabby was still snoring. She knew how to sleep better than anyone in the house.

I started to flip through the pages. Jewish reincarnation was confusing. Math was my least favorite subject and there was a lot of math involved. All the souls in the world came from Adam, who had 248 spiritual organs and limbs and 365 spiritual sinews, whatever those are. The book said his left shoulder alone could be divided into 600,000 souls. And there were five kinds of souls, from low souls to high souls, and each one had to do 613 commandments or they had to get reincarnated again. Plus everyone's name had a number—Adam's name was worth forty-five points, and Eve's name was worth nineteen, and the difference between them was twenty-six, which was one of the names of God. I wanted to know how many points my own name had, but I couldn't figure out the equation.

The book said some weird things about girls, too. Like girl souls can't be reincarnated, only boy souls, because girls go to hell when they die but boys don't because they study the Torah. I didn't like this thought, even though Tabby and Roberta and I wouldn't go to hell because our souls used to be boys. But we might have trouble having babies, the book said, because if a girl has a boy soul, she can't get pregnant unless a girl soul comes in, too. But how could that happen if girl souls couldn't get reincarnated at all? Plus it would be weird to have two souls in one body. Maybe that was what happened with those crazy people who heard voices in their heads. Not having babies was the least of my worries, though. I had to grow up in order to have babies. If I made it to adulthood, I could always adopt.

Also, the book said that if a baby or child dies, it means that their soul has done all 613 commandments and doesn't need to hang around. But my Willie soul died young, and here I was again.

Tabby made a little groan and sat up, blinking her eyes, her hair bunched into clumps. "The man fell out of the balloon," she said, her voice froggy, "and his head came off." That made as much sense as anything I had been reading. I crawled from my bed to Tabby's and wrapped my arms around her. Static sucked our thin nightgowns from our skin, tenting the fabric, making it cling together. It made a crackling sound when I pulled away from her again and let her sleep some more. The book said that soul mates know each other right away. I knew that Tabby was mine.

We missed a lot of movement events. A mass meeting at the Warren Avenue Baptist Church. A vigil in front of Parker & Finney Realtors in Belmont-Cragin where 180 police showed up to protect 500 demonstrators, but people threw bricks and bottles anyway. A mass meeting at New Friendship on the South Side (although that one was on WVON. My dad and I listened at Honest ABE's, a transistor radio perched on the arm of my dad's recliner as I lay on a tweedy couch beside him and Tabby ran around the store.) People debated whether nonviolence could really work. Most people there loved the idea and wanted to keep using it, but a lot of others thought the movement couldn't be so passive when there was so much hatred thrown in their face.

"It's working," my dad said to the radio, rocking his body against the pillowy back of his chair. "If Carla can get gang members to stay nonviolent even when bottles are smacking them in the nose, it's working already."

The meeting got pretty heated—lots of loud voices and crackly static came through the little holes of the radio. I was glad we weren't in the church surrounded by yelling people, even more glad we hadn't been on the streets when bricks flew through the air. The newspapers were getting pretty heated, too. My dad had shown me articles in the *Tribune* and *Sun Times* calling for Dr. King to stop the marches, blaming him for all the violence in the city. Dr. King wouldn't stop, though. He was sure nonviolence would work, sure that all the marchers would show people how to change the world. Or at least parts of Chicago. My dad wrote letters to the editor, kept in touch with Carla, bought more Parker House sausages, but I could tell he wanted to get back into the fray. The Lincoln part of him was rising up inside, wanting to free everyone.

A big march was scheduled in Gage Park for the next day, Saturday. My dad thought he could trick my mom by telling her he was going to take me to a matinee of *Torn Curtain*, but then she said that movie wasn't appropriate for children, plus she wanted to see it herself, so maybe she and my dad should go on a date. Better yet, she said, why don't we all do something together as a family? We hadn't done anything as a family for a while.

I don't think I'd ever been so glad for my mom before. The march worried me. I didn't trust my ability to protect my dad in the face of so many projectiles. We all ended up going to see *Lt. Robin Crusoe, U.S.N.*, at the Tivoli Theater, and even though theaters made me nervous, it felt a lot more safe than a march. It wasn't quite the day of family together-ness that my mom had hoped for, though.

My dad kept talking through the whole movie. In it, Dick Van Dyke is stranded on an island, and he tells the native women that women shouldn't have to marry someone just because their dad tells them to, and then my dad started talking out loud about how the women were going to start a movement on the island and all it takes is one person with a good idea to save the world, just like Dr. King or Dick Van Dyke. My mom kept trying to shush him, and people around us kept trying to shush him, and Roberta found some friends and went to sit with them because she was so embarrassed, and Tabby peeled a piece of gum off the bottom of the seat (but at least she didn't eat it), and I kept looking around for lone gunmen, and by the time we left the theater, all of us were exhausted and cranky and frustrated. We went to The Last Word chicken restaurant for dinner, and ate our cinnamon rolls and our breasts and wings and drumsticks and potatoes, and we barely had any words for each other, much less last ones.

Later that evening, my dad pulled me aside. "I just talked to Carla," he said. "It's a good thing we weren't at that march."

"What happened?" I asked.

"Dr. King got hit in the head with a rock as soon as he got out of his car," he said.

I felt queasy. "Is he okay?"

"He was a little dazed, but he kept marching," my dad said. "People were yelling 'kill the witch doctor' but he kept marching."

"Maybe he should start wearing a helmet," I said.

"They were throwing bricks, firecrackers. Carla even saw a knife or two."

"I don't think we should go to any more marches, Daddy," I said.

"You're probably right, Mina," he said. "At least not in the city. But we can organize here, just like I talked about."

I had hoped that he had forgotten about that. "I don't know," I said. If he was going to pursue this, I might insist he invest in a full set of hockey gear—helmets, pads, the works. Bulletproof, if possible.

"We can't have a meeting here, much less a march," my mother scoffed when he shared his idea with her the next morning. "Remember, this is Downers Grove we're talking about."

"This town has a long history of social justice, Margie." My dad stood up from the table and started to pace around the kitchen.

"This town has a long history of social etiquette, too, Al. . . ."

"Is it social etiquette that only two percent of the black workers at the Argonne Labs can find housing in this area?" my dad shouted. "Is it social etiquette that not even two percent of the Downers Grove population is Negro?"

"You're getting yourself too worked up about this," my mom said.

"Of course I'm getting myself worked up about this!" my dad said. "Everyone should get worked up about this!"

"No one wants any trouble here," my mom said.

"Downers Grove was a station in the Underground Railroad, Margie—the last stop before Chicago! Can you imagine what would have happened if people sent slaves back to the South because no one wanted any trouble? This town led slaves to freedom! Margie, this very house could have been a safe haven for slaves!"

"This is a Sears catalog house, and you know it." My mom slammed the newspaper onto the table and stormed out of the room.

My dad continued to pace. Then he noticed me standing in the pantry.

"Mina! Did you know the former president of Sears was a civil rights activist?"

I knew this was what he wanted to tell my mom if she hadn't run off, but I would let him tell me, anyway. I stepped out from the shadows, holding a large can of peaches in both hands.

"He was. And he was probably president when our house was built," my dad said. "This house has freedom hammered into each plank—I know it! I was reading this book by Carl Sandburg about the Chicago race riots of 1919. . . ."

Shivers went down my arms. Carl Sandburg also wrote a book about Lincoln. A bunch of books about Lincoln. And my dad was reading his books. That had to mean something. I could feel the peaches slosh inside the can, as if they were already inside my stomach.

"Things haven't changed much since then, I'm sorry to say. But the president of Sears was trying to change things at the time. He built hundreds of schools in the country for poor black children. And he was upset about slum conditions in Chicago. He wanted to make things better for the Negroes. Just like Dr. King!"

"That's nice," I said, even though I knew he probably wouldn't even hear me, he was so caught up in his own talk.

"And I think he may have even been Jewish, too. His name was something like Rosenberg or Rosenwald—"

"I think I'm going to eat breakfast, Daddy." I walked over to the refrigerator to get the cottage cheese.

There were so many Sears houses in Downers Grove because the village used to be at the end of a train line. We learned about it at Avery Coonley when we were studying local history. We also learned about Downers Grove being part of the Underground Railroad. I used to imagine that meant there was a real underground train, like a subway. I was upset when I found out most of the slaves had to walk, after all that work they already had to do. They should have been sitting in comfy velvet train seats putting their feet up and looking out the window at all the land they didn't have to plow, not walking miles and miles in the hot sun.

"We're having a meeting," my dad said. "If not at our house, then at the store."

"Will Phyllis let us?" I asked, putting the cottage cheese on the counter.

"Phyllis doesn't own the store," my dad said. "I do."

THE LINCOLN LOG
AN HONEST ABE'S PUBLICATION

Issue 4

Mina Edelman, Editor in Chief

Tabby Edelman, Assistant Editor

Albert Edelman, Consultant

HONEST ABE'S SUPPORTS
THE CHICAGO FREEDOM
MOVEMENT. . . . DO YOU?

If not, what are you afraid of?

Abraham Lincoln said:

"But it is dreaded that the freed people will swarm forth, and cover the whole land! Are they not already in the land? Will liberation make them any more numerous? Equally distributed among the whites of the whole country, and there would be but one colored to seven whites. Could the one, in any way, greatly disturb the seven? There are many communities now, having more than one free colored person to seven whites; and this, without any apparent consciousness of evil from it."

See? There is nothing to worry about. And the ratio between white people and black people in Downers Grove is more like a thousand to one. It doesn't make any sense to be afraid. Or to put a rock through our window. That is just plain stupid. Not to mention expensive for us to clean up. So stop it, please! Be a more decent human being! And come to our meeting on August 10!

By the way, did you know you can get a great deal on lampshades at Honest ABE's? And our armchairs are all on sale (because they got covered with broken glass. The glass is gone now, and we pass the savings on to you)!

Here is another quote from old Abe himself (the real one, not the furniture one):

"There is no reason in the world why the negro is not entitled to all the natural rights enumerated in the Declaration of Independence,--the right to life, liberty, and the pursuit of happiness. I hold that he is as much entitled to these as the white man."

(He gave this speech in Ottawa, IL, in 1858. So we in IL should listen to him still, right? And that means here in Downers Grove, too. And everywhere else. Shouldn't things have gotten better in 108 years?! Come to the meeting on August 10, and we'll talk about it!)

Don't forget to tell your friends about the great furniture deals at Honest ABE's! We sell to anyone of any color. Even green!

Nine people showed up to the meeting, not counting me and my dad. Three scientists from the Argonne Labs and one of their wives. My second-grade teacher, Mr. Elkhart, who I kind of had a crush on when I was in his class. He was younger than the other teachers and knew how to play the harmonica and brought in the best cookies every Friday. He even made them himself. One grandmother-type woman. Two college students—a boy and a girl who both had long hair and held hands the whole night. One nun who just wore the head thing, not the full penguin costume, and a big cross hanging around her neck.

My dad put a leaf in a dining table and we sat around it like we were in someone's house—someone who really liked furniture and had tons of it scattered around. My dad wanted to cook a batch of Parker House sausages and cut them up and serve them on toothpicks for snacks, but since the meeting was after dinnertime, I suggested we get some dessert instead. We picked up a platter of cookies at the Busy Bee Bakery; my dad toted along a carton of Joe Louis Milk. (Our fridge was full of it—I hoped we'd be able to drink it before it turned sour.) If I had known Mr. Elkhart was going to be there, I would have gotten something other than cookies. Nothing could compare to his, not even an assortment of the Busy Bee's best.

"Mina Edelman," Mr. Elkhart said, and shook my hand like I was a real grown-up. "Great job with the newsletter."

My face turned hot.

"I always knew you would do something interesting with your life," he said.

My face turned even hotter, but I was happy. I could die the next day and be okay with it—Mr. Elkhart thought I had done something interesting!

The meeting was kind of boring at first, compared to the meetings in Chicago. Everyone was very polite and kind of calm, although the college students were all wound up and excited.

"It's about time someone makes a difference in this town!" the boy said, and my dad beamed.

"I'm glad to see Democrats here who aren't just Daley Democrats," said one of the scientists. "Seems to me most of the Democrats in DuPage County are part of the white-flight movement."

"They'll pay lip service to open housing but don't want it in their backyard," said another scientist.

"But we do," said the college girl. "We want it in our front yard!"

And then all the other people started getting excited, too, especially Mr. Elkhart, who kept winking at me and banging his hands on the table the way he did on his desk when he was teaching us about something he loved. They made plans for more meetings. Plans for a march. Plans to bring some black people into town for real estate testing. They inhaled the cookies and the Joe Louis milk, especially after my dad told them it was a black-owned brand, and they got more and more convinced that they were going to save Downers Grove.

Just as things were winding down, a couple of men stormed into the store. I recognized one of them—he fixed watches and clocks in a little shop down the street. He sat in the window like an animal in a zoo and people could watch him work with his tiny tools.

"What the hell is going on here?" he asked. It didn't seem like a watch fixer should talk like that.

"We're having the first meeting of the Downers Grove Freedom Movement," my dad said.

"I hear you wanna bring darkies into this town?" The

other man walked toward the table, chomping on a cigar. I recognized him—he worked in the lumberyard across the tracks behind our house.

"Anyone who wants to live here should be able to live here," my dad said.

"Not in my neighborhood," the lumberman said. He spit a brownish puddle on the table in front of my dad.

"That's my merchandise, sir," my dad said. "I'm going to have to ask you to leave."

"No," the watch fixer said. "We're going to have to ask *you* to leave."

Both of the men started toward my dad. I felt frozen. I knew I should protect him, but I didn't know how. The men were huge.

"Oh, no, you don't," Mr. Elkhart said, pushing back his chair and standing up. I yelled, "No!" When the men saw me, they looked like they lost a bit of their nerve. And then they noticed the nun, too.

"Sorry, sister," the watch man said. "I didn't see you."

She frowned at them mercilessly.

"We don't want any trouble in this town," the other man said. "Understand?"

"We understand, all right," my dad said. "We understand that you are both ignoramuses."

"Right on," the college boy said. His girlfriend nodded encouragingly.

"Daddy," I said under my breath, not wanting him to upset the men.

"Please leave," the nun said, and they did, but not

without slamming the glass door on the way out, and yelling "Downers Grove is white! White!" before they ran down the street.

When we got home, my mom glared at my dad.

"I got a call from Mrs. Peterson," she said. "I hear you caused quite a disturbance."

"Some yahoos caused a disturbance," my dad said. "Not us. The only thing we're trying to disturb is the status quo."

"Well, you're disturbing me," my mom said, her voice louder. "I don't know who you are anymore, Al."

"I know who I am for the first time in my life!" my dad said back, his voice louder, too.

They started shouting all sorts of words at one another. I slipped past them and went to commiserate with Tabby, but she was already asleep, so I tiptoed over to Roberta's room and peeked my head inside her door. She was reading a bright pink book—*Valley of the Dolls*. When she saw me, she hid the book under her pillow.

"What do *you* want?" she asked.

"I don't know," I said.

"Then get out of here!" Her face was flushed.

I stood in the doorway for a moment. "Roberta—," I started.

Our parents were still yelling at each other downstairs; I couldn't make out the words, just the loudness.

She looked at me as if she were waiting for me to drop dead on the spot. If she wanted to kill me with her eyes right then, it might have worked.

I took a deep breath. "If Mom and Dad split up," I said, "who would you want to live with?"

"I don't have to worry about that," she said. "I'm going to college."

"Nursing school."

"Same thing," she said.

I couldn't figure out why Roberta wanted to be a nurse—it's not like she liked to help people. She had been more invested in the Future Homemakers of America club than the Future Nurses of America club at school. Maybe she wanted to be a nurse so she could boss people around and tell them they weren't taking enough pills or changing their bandages as often as they should.

"You might as well come in if you're just going to stand there, Mina." She sat up straighter against her headboard. I came in and sat down at the foot of the bed.

"Do you think they're going to split up?" I asked.

"I don't know." She sighed and tipped her head back.

"They're yelling more than ever," I said.

"I know," she said.

"I don't know what to do," I said.

If Roberta heard me, she didn't register it. She just looked wistful and said, "Everything was so much better before."

"Before we started with the movement?" I asked, feeling a little guilty.

"Yeah, that, for sure," she said. "But even before that. Before you were born."

"Gee, that's nice," I said. I wanted to punch her in the mouth.

"Before the baby died." Her voice was softer this time.

"What are you talking about?" I wasn't sure my heart was still beating. My fist opened back up.

"The baby that died before you were born."

I felt shivery all over. So there was an Eddie, after all! "Do you know the baby's name?"

"No, I don't know the baby's name! It wasn't even a baby yet! Mom flushed it down the toilet. I saw it. It was disgusting."

"What did it look like?"

"God, Mina! I don't want to talk about it."

I pictured a clump of raw steak, a miniature red octopus, a tiny doll covered in blood. It was bad enough to flush a dead goldfish down the toilet. How could you flush your own baby? Poor Eddie! Or Edie, maybe, if the baby was a girl.

"Mom was so depressed. She didn't want to play with me. She didn't let me play outside because she thought I'd get hit by a car or something. And then you were born a year later and she was happy again. You could do no wrong, Mina. Mom and Dad let you do anything you wanted. Tabby, too. It's like they were totally different parents to you. I got the strict parents—you got the fun ones." Little bits of spit flew out of her mouth as she talked.

"They're not much fun now."

"So now you know what it's like. God, I can't wait to get out of here!"

"You're not worried about nurse murderers anymore?"

"They caught the guy, Mina."

"But there could be others."

"Did I say you could be in my room?" Roberta pulled a pillow to her chest. "Go!"

My parents were still shouting at each other. I climbed into Tabby's narrow bed and snuggled up against her warm back. I don't know if Tabby was actually asleep, but she turned over and wrapped her arms around me tightly. I could feel something wet on her cheek when she pressed it to mine— drool or tears, I wasn't sure. One set of footsteps pounded up the stairs and then the bedroom door slammed shut across the hall. I could hear my dad sigh downstairs.

Our couches weren't very comfortable for sleeping on— the white leather one in the living room was flat and covered with white leather buttons that left circles on your skin, and the one in the den had scratchy fabric that made your skin itch, and both of them were kind of skinny and sleek, and my dad was neither of those things. One morning I found him curled up in a blanket on the floor by the TV. Not a very dignified position for the former president of the United States.

After a few days, I could tell my dad wanted to make up with my mom. He looked at her with puppy dog eyes. She looked back with flinty snake eyes, like she was sizing him up, seeing whether her jaws could unhinge enough to accommodate his furry body. Their arguments were getting less loud, though. They brushed against each other every once in a while, reached out to touch each other while they were talking, even though my dad was still sleeping downstairs.

Finally, my mom said, "I'll make you a deal," her voice all sly. Her eyeliner was swooped out from the edges of her eyes; it made her look like an international spy or a movie star. Someone mysterious and hard to resist. Not a snake.

"What kind of deal?" my dad asked, raising one bushy eyebrow.

"You can have your little club here, your little protest group." She leaned toward him, rolled a finger around one of his top shirt buttons, as if she was going to slip it through the hole.

"Mmm hmmm?" He leaned toward her.

She played with the curly chest hair peeking out the top of his shirt. He closed his eyes like a cat being petted. "If you give me control of the store."

The spell broke. "What?" my dad asked, pulling his body away.

"It's a great deal," my mom said. She sat up straight, shoulders pulled back, a queen posing for a portrait. "You'll get to do what you want, and I'll get to do what I want."

"And what's that?" my dad asked, arms folded over his chest now.

"Bring some style to this town," she said. "Italian designers are doing amazing things with Lucite these days. My friends are tired of having to go into Chicago to find interesting furniture."

"Your friends? Tired of shopping in Chicago? That's a laugh riot." The laugh that came out of his mouth sounded more like a cough, one that brings up phlegm.

"A woman should be able to run a business in her own town, don't you think?"

"Of course." My dad looked stung, as if he couldn't believe she would have to ask such a thing.

"And a man should be able to run a protest in his own town, yes?" Her voice turned into a purr.

I could see my dad soften to her. His arms dropped to his sides.

My mom fished a few dollars out of her pocket and handed them to me. "Why don't you and Tabby go into town and get some ice cream," she said. "Your dad and I have some things to discuss."

By the time we returned from Feeb's (which had the best Italian ices), my mom was the brand-new proprietress of Mod Margaret's Furnishings.

This was a surprise, to say the least.

"You're closing Honest ABE's?" I asked, trying not to panic.

"I have more important things to work on," he said. "We can dip into our retirement to get by while your mom establishes herself. It's a great opportunity to focus on the movement—"

"What about the *Lincoln Log*?" I could feel tears gurgle in my throat.

My dad looked stricken, as if he hadn't thought about that part of the deal. "Well, Mina, my sweet journalist ballerina . . ." I could tell he was stalling. "Maybe you could do *Mod Magazine* or something of that sort. I'm sure your mother would be thrilled to have a paper at her store."

He seemed happy with this solution, but the look on my mom's face told me it was never going to happen. Besides, the paper wouldn't be the same without Abe. What could I possibly write about white plastic furniture? "Want furniture that looks like it was made in outer space? Check out our uncomfortable chairs!" I felt like someone had ripped out an important part of me, like my larynx or my spleen.

My dad cleared his throat. "I have some more good news," he said. "Thomas is going to move in with us for the rest of the summer."

Tabby started to jump up and down.

"Where's he going to stay?" I didn't want to have to give up my paper *and* my room.

"The mother-in-law apartment over the garage," my dad said. My mom forced herself to smile.

"Shouldn't you call it a stepson apartment, then?" I asked, and my mom's smile fell right off her face. I didn't know why she was so upset—she didn't have a mother-in-law, and my dad had a stepmother-in-law who would never want to live anywhere west of Lake Shore Drive, so it's not like Thomas was going to displace any rightful occupants. The apartment was like our second attic—a storage space for all our old toys and the furniture my mom got sick of. I couldn't figure out why Thomas would want to live there, but I was glad to have something to keep my mind off the imminent demise of the *Lincoln Log*.

"It's like a cultural exchange," my dad told me later. "Carla and I talked about you moving in with her while Thomas was here, but your mother wouldn't have it. No way was she going to let you stay in that neighborhood."

I was relieved. How could I protect my family if I was thirty miles away?

"Plus, Thomas has been having some issues with the local gangs—they want him to get involved and he doesn't want anything to do with them. It's causing some problems for him and Carla."

"Even though she works with them?"

"Afraid so, Mina," my dad said. "So she thought it would do Thomas good to have a little break, and he can help me move the furniture out of the store and make a little money. Not too many jobs in his neighborhood."

"Can I help?" If my stepbrother was going to make money, I should be able to, too.

"Plus, he can help out with our movement activities, and bring some color into our town. It's like a different form of testing."

"If you say so," I said.

"Hopefully we'll wake Downers Grove up," he said.

"We'll make it Uppers Grove," I said. Maybe that could be my new newspaper—*The Uppers Grove Gazette*. It could be about all the good things in the area, all the things people were doing to make our town a better place. And I could reach an even wider audience—maybe Honest ABE's closing could be an opportunity for me, too.

"I don't think we want to wake it up that much." He laughed, and I filed the newspaper idea away in my brain for the time being. I had heard some of Roberta's friends make jokes about uppers and downers before, and I knew they were talking about pills, but I didn't know what the pills did to you. It was amazing to me that medicine could make you feel up or down, that it could take pain away or stop a heart attack or infection in any part of your body. It was like magic. Maybe when Roberta was a nurse, I could ask her for some uppers or downers so I could see what they felt like.

Roberta probably wouldn't have said yes to any of my requests that day, though. She was not happy about the idea of a black boy coming to live above our garage.

"What will my friends say?" she asked.

"Thomas is nice," I told her, even though I didn't really know him enough to say that. It just seemed like I should try to defend my sort-of brother.

"He's right around your age, Roberta," my dad said. "You can show him the town."

"No way," Roberta said. "No way am I going to be seen escorting him around. My friends would flip out."

"Then maybe you should find some better friends," my dad said. "I expect all of you to welcome Thomas and treat him like family."

"He likes white people music," I said.

Roberta made one of her exasperated sighs. "Mom?" she said. "Do I have to put up with this?"

"He's going to be here less than a month. As are you. I think we can all manage a little hospitality."

"You're getting a store out of it!" Roberta yelled. "What am I getting?"

"A lesson in tolerance," my dad said. "A lesson in civility."

"Maybe you should try showing more civility to your daughter who's going to be leaving forever!" Roberta shouted and stormed out of the room. My mom threw a look at my dad as if to say "look what you've done now."

We picked up Thomas at the train station a couple of days later. My mom and Roberta didn't want to go, but my dad told my mom it was part of the agreement. If she wanted the store, she and Roberta had to be there for Thomas's arrival. My mom, who had already begun to order furniture from Italy and Denmark and New York, didn't have much of a choice.

Roberta blanched. "But why do I have to be there?" she whined.

"We want him to know the entire family welcomes him," my dad said. "It's the least you can do, Roberta."

Roberta didn't even look at Thomas as he got off the train, a battered suitcase in one hand, a guitar case in the other—she was too busy looking around, gauging everyone else's reaction on the platform. Thomas looked at her, though—I could see his eyes light up. My dad gave Thomas a hearty hug, his hands clapping against Thomas's back, making Thomas cough. My mom put on her cheery out-in-the-world smile. "Glad to meet you, Thomas," she said. "Thank you for coming out to help us."

"Thank you, ma'am," Thomas said, looking down. He snuck another quick look at Roberta, but she didn't notice.

"Hi, Thomas," I said quietly, and he nodded.

"Thomas, Thomas, he's our boy," Tabby yelled, "if he can't do it, flim flam floy!"

Thomas flinched, and my dad quickly said, "Thomas is not our boy," to Tabby. "Thomas is his own man." I thought Thomas might start to laugh at this grand pronouncement, but he seemed glad that my dad said it.

All the people on the platform, much to Roberta's chagrin, were staring at Thomas, staring at us. Some of them not just staring but scowling. It wasn't often that a black person came into town, especially one carrying a guitar. My dad pretended no one else was there but our family.

"Welcome, welcome, welcome to Downers Grove," my dad said. "Let me take your bags to the car."

"I can carry them, sir," Thomas said in his deep voice. Roberta glanced over at him quickly, then looked away again. She pretended to read a train schedule, probably so people would think she wasn't with us.

"No, no, I insist," my dad said loudly. I could tell he wanted people to hear him, which made Roberta shrink into herself even more. "*I'll* be *your* porter today."

"I've never been a porter, sir," Thomas said softly.

My dad tried to take the bags from his hands, but Thomas held on to them tight. Eventually he let go of his suitcase, but he wouldn't let my dad carry his guitar.

We loaded his stuff into the trunk and squeezed into my mom's car. Tabby sat on the front seat between our parents, and Thomas, based on my dad's advice, sat in between me and Roberta in the back. Roberta squished herself over to the very side of the seat and pressed her face to the window so no part of her would touch any part of Thomas. Sometimes, though, we rounded a corner and Thomas bumped into either Roberta or me. Once we took a turn so hard, he was pressed against Roberta for a good long while.

"Excuse me, miss," he stammered after he could sit up again. Roberta flushed bright red.

"Roberta," she said, and he smiled a secret sort of smile.

"I'll give you the scenic tour," my dad said. "The lay of the land."

We drove through the downtown village—my dad pointed out Honest ABE's and Mochel's Hardware and Feeb's and the Busy Bee and all the other little stores he might (or probably might not) be interested in.

"The Rexall has a soda fountain," my dad said. "They should let you sit there, I imagine."

Thomas's face clouded.

"If they don't," my dad said, "they have me to reckon with."

He drove us down Ogden, past the Tops Big Boy car place and the Last Word and other restaurants and businesses. He took us all the way to the Morton Arboretum, where we drove through thousands of acres of trees and plants from all around the world. I had been to the Morton Arboretum many times—at least once a year for a school field trip and other times for picnics and birthday parties—so it didn't seem like that big a deal to me, but Thomas kept catching his breath, and sometimes I heard him whisper what sounded like "beautiful." That made Roberta blush, too. We drove past the section with all the trees and gardens from Japan, and the China section and the Ozarks section, the olive family section and the cashew family and the elm family and the pine family and the flowering trees, and Thomas kept shaking his head as if he'd never seen anything so amazing in his life. I wanted to tell him that it was just trees, just green, but it seemed like he was seeing something more than that.

We drove to the Graue Mill and Museum, an old building where farmers used to grind wheat and corn in the 1800s, another field-trip staple. I looked at my family to see if they recognized anything from our old life—the style of furniture, the kitchenware, the lack of electricity—but I couldn't tell if it was registering with them. Tabby, who had fallen asleep in the car at the arboretum, was running around, touching things she wasn't supposed to touch. It turned out the college girl from the meeting worked there—she was dressed in clothes from the time period and demonstrating how to spin wool into yarn. She looked right at home in her nineteenth-century dress, her pale skin and long hair making her look like a beautiful girl in an old story who dies of consumption. She probably lived back then, too. She took Tabby aside and showed her how the wool felt, how it felt different after it was spun. Sort of like the Lincolns spun into the Edelmans—the same material in a different form.

"You might be interested in this, Mr. Edelman," the girl said. "Abraham Lincoln came through here once on a trip from Chicago to Springfield."

I felt myself wake up a notch—maybe she had some window into our life back then—until she said, "With the name of your store and all."

Then she noticed Thomas, who had been standing behind my dad in a shadowy corner of the room near a bunch of spindles. She stepped away from her spinning wheel and rushed at him, beaming as if he was some sort of celebrity.

"This is Thomas," my dad said. "He'll be staying with us the rest of the summer."

"Cindy," the girl said, pumping Thomas's hand. "It's so wonderful to have you here."

Thomas looked a little embarrassed but smiled at Cindy anyway, right into her eyes. It was hard to believe, but Roberta looked kind of jealous about this. She glared at Cindy as if she thought Cindy was trying to steal her boyfriend.

"This mill used to be a stop in the underground railroad, you know," Cindy said, nodding earnestly. "Mr. Graue used to hide slaves in the basement."

"Don't worry," Thomas said. "I was never a slave." Cindy flushed. Roberta looked strangely triumphant.

"Of course." Cindy stammered a bit. "But I thought you'd like to know. Those of us in the movement take it as a source of pride."

As my dad and Cindy talked about the movement, Thomas stood there, alternately looking at the floor and looking at Cindy. Tabby and I went to grind corn while my mom and Roberta headed to the gift shop. I tried to see if I could feel any Lincoln molecules in the air—I took a deep breath, but all I could smell was dust and cornmeal and wood. When I sneezed, the sneeze felt like it went all the way down to my toes, so maybe a few Lincoln atoms were shivering their way through me.

In the car on the way home, Roberta didn't say a word to Thomas, but she didn't press herself against the window this time, and I could tell she didn't mind so much when we turned a corner and he tipped against her.

"That Cindy is a nice girl, isn't she?" my dad said. "A sociology major at Northwestern. Her boyfriend, too. Good to see young people getting into the social sciences these days, isn't it?"

Thomas's face dropped a little at the mention of Cindy's boyfriend. Roberta's face lit up.

"I got the most darling corn bread tins," my mom said, rummaging in the bag from the gift shop. "Cast iron, shaped like little ears of corn. And some fresh cornmeal. Maybe we can make corn bread tonight. Would you like that, Thomas?"

"You shouldn't assume Thomas likes Southern cooking just because he's black, Margie," my dad said in a scolding tone. My mom scowled at him.

"I love corn bread, Mrs. Edelman," Thomas said. "Thank you."

"You're very welcome, Thomas." My mom put her public face back on. Then she turned to my dad and said, "It's not as if I suggested watermelon."

Thomas and my dad both sighed.

"Watermelon, watermelon, in a dish, how many pieces do you wish?" Tabby started to chant. We usually said "bubblegum," not "watermelon," for the jump rope rhyme. I liked that one a lot better than "Lincoln, Lincoln, I been thinkin', what the heck have you been drinkin'? Looks like water, tastes like wine, oh my gosh, it's turpentine!" I had cleared all the turpentine out of our garage, just in case.

"That's enough, Tabby," my dad said.

"One, two, three, four, five, six!" Tabby said, jumping a little higher on the front seat with each new number. She probably would have kept going, but then my dad put a hand on her shoulder and pushed her gently back down onto the seat.

Thomas seemed to like his new home. He had one big room over the garage, with a couch that pulled out into a bed—one of our mom's old couches, not terribly comfortable, but a little more so than the ones in our house—and our old TV set and some other alien furniture, plus a little fake kitchen on one side of the room with a tiny fridge and a sink and a hotplate, and a little bathroom in the back with a shower stall and a toilet.

"You're welcome to join us for meals," my dad said.

"Just knock on the kitchen door," my mom said. My dad had wanted to give Thomas the keys to our house, but my mom wouldn't go for that.

"We'll probably dine at six," my mom said, "if you want to wash up first."

"Thank you," Thomas said. He repositioned his guitar case, which was slipping sideways against the wall. It looked even more alien than the furniture in the room. No one in our family was musical, aside from our record collection, and that was a strange mix of opera (my mom's, but she barely listened to them unless we had a dinner party), show tunes (Tabby and I liked to act out scenes from *My Fair Lady* and *South Pacific* and *The King and I*), crooners (my dad's favorites until he started listening to Mahalia Jackson and Nina Simone), and poppy stuff (Roberta spent most of her allowance on her records—sometimes Tabby and I would sneak into her room and dance to her albums if she wasn't home).

My mom brought out the opera for dinner that night—she probably wanted Thomas to think we were very civilized white people. The record was filled with a lot of angry-sounding singing and dramatic swells of music. That probably showed Thomas more what it was like in our house than my mom would have liked. The record's volume was way too high for much conversation. My dad tried to speak loudly about his attempt to bring the movement to Downers Grove, but he kept getting drowned out by cymbals. Thomas and Roberta kept sneaking looks at each other over their plates of corn bread and pot roast, but neither of them said a word to each other. Thomas's thank yous to my parents were about as regular as the tympanis on the album. My mom finally turned off the music before dessert, but by then our ears were ringing and we didn't say much over our dishes of rainbow sherbet.

Thomas gave Carla a call in the kitchen before he headed back to the mother-in-law apartment. He talked too softly for me to understand him. My dad got on after he did and said, "So good to have your son here. A fine, fine young man." He smiled the way he only did when he talked to

Carla. A sort of dreamy, hopeful smile. I wondered if my mom was bothered by this smile at all, but she didn't seem to notice. She was too busy washing out her new corn bread tins, trying to get all the caked-on gunk out of the corn kernel–shaped dips.

As I was going to sleep later, "Blowing in the Wind" blew into my open window—Thomas playing it on his guitar, his own window open. He was singing, but not like Bob Dylan's whine. His voice was low and deep and slow. I could feel it rumble in my chest.

"Is that song about passing gas?" Tabby asked.

"No, you silly," I said. "It's a very serious song."

"I just blew wind," Tabby said, giggling.

It was a warm evening, but I pulled my comforter up over my sheet. I didn't like what the song was saying. That we didn't know the answers to anything. That it was all blowing in the air around us. That there was nothing very solid for us to hold on to. I grabbed my thigh, just to make sure I was still there.

THE LINCOLN LOG
AN HONEST ABE'S PUBLICATION

Issue 5

Mina Edelman, Editor in Chief

Tabby Edelman, Assistant Editor

Albert Edelman, Consultant

HONEST ABE'S CLOSING DOWN!
EVERYTHING MUST GO!

Honest ABE's is closing its doors to make way for a
great new store--Mod Margaret's Furnishings. Your
house will look like a spaceship by the time you're
done shopping at Mod Margaret's!

But we can't leave without giving you some great
savings and without letting you know a little bit
more about the Lincolns and their furniture.

In their Springfield house, the Lincolns had a lot
of whatnots. I had never heard of a whatnot before,
so I asked my dad (the ABE of Honest ABE's) what a
whatnot was, and he said, "What is a whatnot not?"
He's a joker. But then he said that it was like a
little curio cabinet. So if you want a whatnot, get
one of our curio cabinets before they're all gone,
or you'll say, "Why did I not get a whatnot?"

When Abe was our great president, the Lincolns spent
their summers at the Soldiers' Home, about four
miles away from the White House. Actual soldiers who
got hurt in the war were there. They were all bloody
and moaning, so I don't see why that would be a
great vacation spot, but the Lincolns sure loved it.
Every year, they packed up about twelve trucks full
of White House furniture and sent it to the
Soldiers' Home. At the end of their stay, they sent
it back again. I guess Mary didn't want to be
separated from her fancy furniture after she spent
so much of the country's money on it.

Here's the funny thing, though: When Mary and Tad and Robert left the White House after Abe was killed, they only took one piece of furniture with them--a little dressing stand that Abe liked a lot. When he was alive, he told Mary that if the commissioner said it was okay, he would like to take that stand back to Springfield with him. So Mary asked, and the commissioner said it was okay, and she had it shipped to Chicago, where Tad used it as a desk. Tad had always been a very bad student and could barely read or write, but with that desk, he started to do better in school. Maybe the desk was magic. Are the desks we sell at Honest ABE's magic? Buy one and see for yourself! There's not much time left, so you better hurry!

Thank you for being an Honest ABE's customer (but if you threw a rock through the window or got mad at our signs, we take back those thanks). Be sure to give Mod Margaret's a go!

My dad was hoping to sell every stick of furniture in the store by the time Honest ABE's closed for good, but we weren't quite that lucky.

"Maybe more customers will come if you take the END RACISM signs out of the window," Phyllis said nervously.

"I won't do that," my dad said. "Even if I lose thousands of dollars, I will not compromise my integrity."

The BLACK CUSTOMERS WELCOME and WE SUPPORT THE CHICAGO—AND DOWNERS GROVE—FREEDOM MOVEMENT and WE SHALL OVERCOME signs stayed up, although, to Phyllis's relief, the 30% OFF and then 50% OFF and then 75% OFF!!!!! signs were much larger. It was the last one that caught people's eyes. We sold about half of the stock after that sign went up.

Thomas spent his days at the store with my dad. He helped write receipts and carry furniture to people's cars or to the delivery truck. When he carried furniture, my dad did, too. He said he didn't want Thomas to feel like a mule, doing all the grunt work by himself while my dad sat at a desk with his hands folded behind his head. If any customer gave Thomas a dirty look, my dad would start to pipe up about what a fine young man Thomas was and wasn't it a shame there weren't more fine young men like Thomas in Downers Grove. More fine young black men would bring some dignity to our town, he said. He lost a few last-minute customers this way. Thomas didn't seem to like it when my dad said things like this, but most of the time he didn't say anything. He usually only said a few words at meals. The most I heard his voice was after everyone went to bed and he sang with his guitar. Some of the songs I recognized, but I think he was making some of them up, too. Especially the one about the girl who wouldn't talk to him but kept casting glances his way. Roberta never said anything about his music, but I heard her humming that song one day when she was doing her hair in the bathroom, and when she came out, she had a silly grin on her face.

I could tell Roberta wanted to talk to Thomas, but nothing more than "please pass the tomatoes" or "thank you" ever came up between them. The way they said those things sounded like they were saying something more underneath, though—something like "I wrote a song about you" and "I heard that song and can't get it out of my head." Sometimes when Roberta had friends over, they would stare at Thomas and then go to her room to whisper and giggle. I was sure Thomas would say one of his spare, cutting sentences to put them in their place, but he didn't. He just shook his head and smiled.

I wanted to talk to Thomas, too, but I didn't know what to say. What do you say to a fake stepbrother who has different-colored skin and doesn't speak much to begin with? Tabby and my dad were really the only people who spent any time with him. I found myself feeling jealous whenever Thomas rode Tabby around on his back or spun her like an airplane. I wanted him to do it to me, but I was too big. And Tabby was getting too big for me to do that to her. I just went to my room to read whenever they started to play together.

My friends had sent me a bunch of letters all summer. I missed them terribly. I wanted to write back saying "Can I come join you? Can you send me a ticket to Camp Minnehaha (or Rome or Boca Raton, as the case may be)? Can you help me get out of this place?" But then I thought about the march, and how much my dad needed me, and I wrote back "Have fun while I'm changing the world!" instead. I'd see my friends soon enough. I could wait; open housing couldn't.

Hollister Burgeron showed up on our doorstep one morning. I was surprised by how happy I was to see him. Tabby was still asleep, and everyone else was busy—my mom out ordering more furniture for her soon-to-open store, my dad and Thomas carting furniture away from the almost-departed Honest ABE's, Roberta off in Robertaland, wherever that might be. I didn't even think to check for weapons before I opened the door.

"Why do you have a nigger at your house?" he asked.

I suddenly wasn't as happy to look at his bucktoothed face.

"He's not a nigger," I said.

"Well, he's not white, that's for sure," Hollister said. He had a slingshot in his back pocket.

"You shouldn't say nigger, you should say colored," I told him. "I mean, black. And you better not be here to shoot him."

"I don't shoot niggers," Hollister said. "I just shoot VC."

"I don't think you'll find any Vietcong in Downers Grove," I said. I felt proud of myself that I knew what the initials meant.

"You never know." Hollister had more freckles than the last time I saw him. His knees looked knobbier, too. "I didn't think I'd find a nigger in your house, neither."

"A black person," I said. "And his name is Thomas."

"You know what I mean," Hollister said. He seemed to be looking at my chest. I crossed my arms to bump his eyes away.

"You should come to our march," I said. "In two Saturdays. Then you'll know why Thomas is here."

Hollister shrugged.

"Did your dad get his hook yet?" I asked.

"Nah," he said.

I wanted to ask him more about his dad—did he learn how to write and wipe himself with his left hand, or did other people have to do it for him? Did he ever dream that he had both arms and get sad when he woke up and remembered one had been blown off? I clutched my crossed arms, glad to have them whole.

"There he is," Hollister said, and I half expected to see his one-armed dad ambling up the front walk. My heart started to hammer at the thought of it—I didn't like the idea of seeing his stump again—but it was just my dad and Thomas, pulling into the driveway in the Honest ABE's truck, a big picture of my dad in his stovepipe hat on the side of it.

"You better be nice, Hollister," I said. "You better not use that slingshot."

"I don't even have a rock," he said. He took the slingshot out of his pocket, pulled back the elastic, and snapped it against my elbow.

I said "Ow," even though it surprised me more than it hurt. I blinked away the tears that popped embarrassingly into my eyes and grabbed the slingshot from his hand.

"Don't you ever hurt me or my family again," I told him. I didn't know how to make the slingshot work, so I just swung it like a Ping-Pong paddle and popped him on the chest with the elastic. It didn't hit him very hard—it was more of a brush than a slap.

"Geez, Mina," he said. "I was just kidding."

"I wasn't," I said and slammed the door in his face.

"Give me back my slingshot!" he yelled through the door.

"Your dad can come and get it when he gets his hook!" I yelled back.

Hollister kicked the door. He watched my dad and Thomas start to unload furniture from the back of the truck for a few seconds before he ran off. The sole of one of his sneakers flapped and I felt a little sorry for him that he had such raggedy shoes. His mom was probably too busy wiping his dad's butt and cleaning his stump to take Hollister shopping for a new pair.

I walked outside and headed over to the truck as soon as Hollister was out of view. My dad was wrestling a large coffee table out of the truck, his face red from exertion.

"Be careful," I told him. "You don't want to get heat-stroke again."

"I don't know," he said, dropping the coffee table to the ground faster than he probably would have liked. "It was pretty enlightening before."

"Be careful," I said again. I picked up one end of the coffee table and helped him carry it to the garage, where Thomas had just stacked three end tables in a Yertle the Turtle–like pile.

Our garage was turning into a miniature Honest ABE's, but with less floor space, the furniture smushed and piled together, not spread out into little fake room settings. It made me claustrophobic to look at chairs sitting on couches, dressers perched on dining room tables, buffets laden with coffee tables and lamps. I worried the furniture wouldn't be able to breathe.

Roberta appeared out of nowhere, all dolled up for ten in the morning, wearing way too much makeup, a turquoise dress with yellow splotches that looked more like lymphocytes (BHAGFMG, p. 137) than anything else, along with yellow kitten heels, her hair piled on top of her head. She looked like a clown version of herself, or maybe a clown version of my mom. From the way he smiled at her, Thomas seemed to think she looked pretty good, but maybe it was because she was holding a tray of lemonade. Roberta had never done anything nice like that before, at least not without being asked, but she teetered over to Thomas and my dad and said, "I thought you two could use a nice cold glass of lemonade, doing all this hard work in the hot sun." She said it really fast, like she had rehearsed it but was getting ahead of herself.

"I'd like some lemonade, Roberta," I said.

"Get your own," she hissed at me. "I only brought two glasses."

"Thank you, sweetheart," my dad said.

"Yes, thank you, Roberta," Thomas said, looking into her eyes as she handed him his glass.

"I'll leave the pitcher out here so you can serve yourselves more when you want," she said. She set the tray on the edge of a dresser, which was precariously perched on top of a stereo console. The tray teetered and the pitcher came crashing to the ground, splashing lemonade everywhere. Roberta gasped and bent to pick up the pieces, and then the dresser wobbled and tipped over and was about to slam right on her head when Thomas dove across the garage and pushed it back up on top of the console where it belonged.

Roberta blinked up at Thomas, her hands full of broken glass. The whole garage smelled like lemons. We were all spattered with juice.

"You saved my life," she said. I could see her back shake as she stayed in her crouched position.

"I just saved you from a nasty headache," he said.

"No," she insisted. She stood up right in front of him, her eyes brimming with tears. "You saved my life."

That night, I looked out the window and saw Roberta creeping across the lawn in her pink robe with the satin ribbon belt. She tiptoed up the stairs over the garage, up to Thomas's room. I saw him open the door, wearing only his pajama bottoms. I couldn't see his face fully in the dark, but I could tell by the way he was standing that he seemed surprised to see her. Happy, too. They stood on the little landing at the top of the stairs for a few moments. Then he put his hand on her shoulder, led her into the mother-in-law apartment, and closed the door behind them. I watched through the window for a pretty long time, but I didn't see her come back out.

At breakfast the next morning, Roberta and Thomas stared at each other across the table. Both of them looked like they were going to bust out laughing any second, they were so full of happiness. They looked at each other the way I sometimes saw my dad and Carla look at each other.

"Pass the salt, please," Roberta said, and Thomas held it out to her, grinning. Their fingers laced together briefly as she took the rectangular Plexiglas shaker.

I think my dad noticed this because he cleared his throat. "Did you sleep well, Thomas?" he asked, crumbs in his beard.

"Very well, sir," he said, looking down at his plate.

"Are you ready to do some more heavy lifting today?"

"Sure am, sir," Thomas said. "Whatever you need me for." He snuck a sideways look at Roberta. She blushed like crazy.

I checked to see if Tabby saw this, too, but she was too busy making a scrambled egg and grape jelly toast sandwich. My mom hadn't noticed, either. She hadn't sat down to eat with us yet. She was standing at the sink scrubbing the egg pan, her elbow moving a million miles an hour. My mom never used to like cleaning, but she had thrown herself into it lately like it was a competitive sport. It seemed to me that should have made my dad glad, but he would just stare at her and shake his head.

"We need to get ready for the march, too," my dad said—he looked at Thomas, and then at me. This time, my mom shook her head.

After breakfast, my dad took Tabby to the speech therapist, and my mom and I went to the store to turn it into Mod Margaret's. She had already pulled up all the carpet, and painted the concrete beneath bright green. Now we were working on painting the walls orange. One wall, at least—she was thinking of one wall blue, and one purple, too. Maybe with some white stripes or polka dots on top. I got orange splotches and splashes all over my shorts and bare legs.

It was weird to be in Honest ABE's without it being Honest ABE's anymore—I could feel the ghosts of the furniture hovering in the big empty room, the ghost of my dad in his Lincoln suit. It felt good to work with my mom, though. When I was little, I spent almost all of my time with my mom, but we had kind of forgotten how to be with each other. I looked over at her running a roller dripping with paint up and down along the wall as fast as she could, and I felt a rush of emotion—I wasn't sure if it was love in my heart or if I was feeling sorry for her tired arm. The paint made the air smell like anxiety.

"Thanks for helping me, sweetie," she said, letting her arm rest for a moment. She had managed to not get a single drip of paint on her tight black pants, her black-and-white striped sheath. A Pucci scarf in lime green and yellow and pink was tied around her hair.

"I wasn't sure you wanted me to," I said.

"Now, why would you say that?" she asked, one hand on her hip. Her nails, I noticed, were polished white. They were as clean as the shells we bought at the Shedd Aquarium.

"I thought you only liked to spend time with Roberta," I said.

My mom sighed. She put down the roller and took my face in her hands.

"Mina," she said, "how could you ever think such a thing?"

"Roberta wears clothes like you," I said. "She takes the skin off her chicken like you."

My mom squeezed my face.

"I don't do those things," I said.

"Honey," my mom said, "Roberta is my mirror. Roberta is like me looking at me. Tabby is more like the wild animal part of me. But you, Mina—you're my heart."

My mom didn't talk about hearts very often. My heart squeezed a little at the sound of it.

"So you like me better than Roberta?" I felt a strange burble of triumph.

"That's not what I mean." She laughed. "And it's not a contest—you should know that, Mina. It's just that you're the me I forget is inside me sometimes. The me I wanted to be when I was a girl."

I realized I had never seen a picture of my mom as a girl. I wondered what she had looked like, what she had acted like. Why she had wanted to be someone like me. Maybe she really wanted to be Willie more than she wanted to be Mina. Maybe I did, too.

"If I die, will you promise that you won't go crazy?" I asked.

"Mina! Where did that come from?"

"Promise me, Mommy, please?"

She pulled back and looked at me like she was mad at me. "I can't promise any such thing. Of course I would go crazy if something happened to you. If something happened to any of you girls."

"Just promise me you won't end up in a nuthouse with a bunch of footstools." I could feel the tears on my cheeks.

"Mina, you're not planning something, are you?"

"Sometimes things happen. . . ." Like typhoid. Like bullets. Like people throwing rocks during protest marches.

"I'm not going to let anything happen to you." She wrapped me up in her arms and rocked me back and forth like a baby, or a crazy person.

Over the next few days, trucks and trucks of furniture started to arrive at the store. Weird clear plastic bubble chairs that hung from the ceiling. Dining room chairs that looked like swoopy white plastic spoons. A sofa made of lots of circle cushions stuck together. Room dividers in primary colors. Everything very bright. Nothing very comfortable. My mom was ecstatic, although she looked a little nervous when she had to sign the delivery men's papers.

My mom planned a big shindig to celebrate the opening. She hired a friend who was trying to start a catering company to make chafing dishes full of Swedish meatballs and pigs in blankets and platters of crudités and caviar on toast points. She hired a bartender to mix drinks. She bought a new stereo system and a bunch of new jazz records—at least she called them jazz, but they sounded like outer space music with all sorts of whirs and eerie singing (which went with the store, so that made sense). She bought a brand-new Pucci dress covered with swirls of brightness and a brand-new pair of tall white boots.

The day of the party, she was pacing around like a

maniac. I heard her tell my dad that she didn't want Thomas to come, and my dad blew his top. He said that if Thomas couldn't go, he wouldn't go, and my mom said fine, she didn't want him there anyway. And then, to my huge shock, Roberta said that if Thomas couldn't go, she wouldn't go, either. And my mom looked very hurt. "Roberta," she said, "I wouldn't have expected that from you." That made two of us. Roberta said, "You don't know everything about me," and stormed out of the room.

My mom let me and Tabby come to the party, even though she told her friends not to bring their kids. She bought us new dresses—miniature versions of hers—and washed our faces and brushed and tied our hair back with thick headbands herself. She even rubbed a little lipstick onto our cheeks to give us a "healthy glow." Her friends showed up in gowns and beehives, their husbands in tuxes. No one else from the town came, so it was a pretty small party. I tried to be civilized and passed around trays of hors d'oeuvres, but Tabby started running around, and eventually I joined her, dodging long skirts and cigarettes and martini glasses and weird furniture. My mom threw us nasty "calm down" looks at first, but eventually she stopped looking our way and spent more time showing off the store and telling her friends where each piece of furniture came from. The room got louder and smokier by the minute. By the end of the night, she had sold one bubble chair and one Eames room divider and she looked exhausted. After the guests were all gone, she took off her shoes and sat on the couch made of circles, smoking a cigarette like a zombie.

"I'm sure more people will come during store hours," she said. But she had put a big notice in the paper about the party and the only people who came were people who knew her. And some of her friends didn't come at all—they had stopped talking to her after Thomas moved in.

"The pigs in blankets were really good," I told her.

"Wienies in sheets!" yelled Tabby. She really pushed the *sh* sound in sheets, the *t* at the end of it. She was getting much better at saying words. About a month before, it would have sounded like *theeth*.

"Thanks for being here, girls," my mom said. "It means a lot to me." And we curled up together in our matching dresses on the uncomfortable couch and tried not to fall off the edge.

Business hours didn't help the store much. A lot of people came in to gawk at the space-age furniture, but no one wanted to buy anything. It didn't fit with the overriding Honest ABE's decor of Downers Grove. My mom was worried. She worried out loud to my dad. She worried to her friends on the phone. To her father, too. To anyone who would listen.

"Business will pick up," my dad said. He didn't want to hear about her worries. He was too busy gearing up for the march. I found him on the phone to one person or another at almost all times, coordinating sign making and meeting places and where to convene afterward. Not to mention what to do if someone gets arrested, what to do if someone throws something at the marchers. *Go limp* seemed to be the main piece of advice. *Don't fight back. We're nonviolent, not violent.*

"What if it doesn't?" she said. "What if I can't pay my loans back, Al?"

"We'll cross that bridge when we come to it," he said, and I could hear Thomas's voice singing "Bridge Over Troubled Water" in my mind.

The day before the march, my dad and Thomas drove the Honest ABE's truck, filled with furniture, to Thomas and Carla's neighborhood. My dad thought he'd just pass it out to whoever wanted it for free, but he told me Carla said the neighborhood didn't want handouts. She told him he could sell it for cheap at the local community center as a fundraiser for the movement. That sounded good to him. So sofas that normally went for seventy dollars sold for five, and two-hundred-dollar dining room sets sold for ten dollars, but it added up to over four hundred dollars all together. That would pay for a lot of signs, plus even some legal fees if people needed them, my dad said. He came home thrilled. Thomas seemed a little distracted—maybe he thought he should have stayed in the city with his mom. Although when he looked at Roberta, he seemed much happier to be in Downers Grove.

Much to my surprise, Roberta came down to breakfast the next morning and said she was going to march with us. My dad had stayed up late using toxic-smelling markers to write "Don't Be a Downer! Open Downers Grove!" and "Be

Fair—Housing for Everyone" on poster board and wasn't quite ready yet. I made my own sign while I ate my cereal.

THERE IS NO REASON IN THE WORLD WHY THE NEGRO IS NOT ENTITLED TO ALL THE NATURAL RIGHTS ENUMERATED IN THE DECLARATION OF INDEPENDENCE,— THE RIGHT TO LIFE, LIBERTY, AND THE PURSUIT OF HAPPINESS. I HOLD THAT HE IS AS MUCH ENTITLED TO THESE AS THE WHITE MAN. —HONEST ABE

I knew it would be hard to read from far away, and the words got kind of squished together at the bottom because I made them too big on the top, but it seemed like the right quote to carry around.

My dad came downstairs in his full Honest ABE garb— the suit, the stovepipe hat, the works.

"Please tell me you are not really wearing that," Roberta said.

"Of course I'm wearing this," my dad said. "Who better to make a point about equality than Lincoln himself?"

My dad had actually been hoping that Dr. King would come out for our march, that a whole contingent of movement people would come out to Downers Grove, but no one was able to. Not even Carla.

The four of us met up with the other marchers—the five people from the meeting, plus six more (three college students, three more grandmas)—in front of the pharmacy. I could see the pharmacist look quizzically out the window at us. I hadn't been in to bother him for a prescription for a while. I waved, and he raised his eyebrows and shook his head at me.

"This is it," my dad said. "Are you ready to change Downers Grove?"

The marchers started to whoop and raise their signs in the air. Roberta and Thomas just stood there smiling at each other, though. They had one sign to hold between them: LOVE THY NEIGHBOR.

Downtown was fairly quiet—at first it didn't seem as if anyone noticed that a clump of fifteen people were walking down the center of Main Street holding signs and chanting, "Free Downers Grove! Free Downers Grove!" Then people started to poke their heads out of the bakery and the Grove Emporium and the shoe shop where you could stick your foot in an X-ray machine and look at your metacarpals.

"You giving something away?" a teenage boy yelled from a parked car. I don't know if he even read the signs. He must have just heard the word *free*.

"We're giving away justice!" my dad yelled back, and the marchers cheered. The boy just shook his head.

More people trickled out of the stores. Some cars started to honk at us for blocking the road.

"No Niggers Grove!" someone yelled from the sidewalk.

Some people from the bakery started throwing long loaves of bread at us, like spears. Day old, probably. The crust was pretty hard when it glanced off my arm, but at least it was unlikely to be lethal. I looked around to make sure no one else was going to throw anything worse.

Mr. Burgeron was sitting on the curb, one sleeve folded and pinned neatly below his stump, an empty Strawberry Crush bottle in his living hand. At least I thought the bottle was empty. As I got closer, I saw a rag was sticking out of it. Hollister was sitting on the curb next to his dad. Both of them stood up when the march got right nearby. I waved at Hollister, but he didn't look at me. He was busy fumbling with a matchbook. His dad leaned toward him, maybe telling him how to do it. Finally, he got a match to light. And he touched it to the rag in the bottle. And Mr. Burgeron cranked his one arm back and tossed the bottle with all his might.

"Molotov cocktail!" someone yelled, and people started screaming.

I had heard the term before, but wasn't sure what it meant. I imagined Strawberry Crush with some alcohol in it, something that burned the throat.

The bottle arced over our heads like a comet and went crashing right through the window of Mod Margaret's. A huge fireball roared out through the broken glass, spitting fire onto the roof. Fire inside the store crackled and flared.

"Mommy!" I screamed. I could see flames licking around the curves of one of the bubble chairs and an Eames room divider collapsing in on itself.

"She's not there," my dad said as we raced away from the flames. The marchers had unclumped; people were running everywhere. Roberta and Thomas ran off together holding hands. "The store is closed today. She's home with Tabby."

"But all the furniture . . ." The smell of smoke, awful fumy plasticky smoke, made me want to gag. I was very relieved Tabby wasn't there to breathe it in.

"We can sacrifice some furniture for the cause," my dad said, huffing and puffing. "It's better than a human life."

"Mr. Burgeron threw the bottle!" I said. "And Hollister!" I should have stopped them. I should have known something was wrong when I saw the rag in the bottle. I should have run over and taken it out of his hand and smashed it on the ground. Sirens started to fill the air.

My dad's face clouded over, but he composed himself. "No vengeance," my dad said. "That's not what we're about."

I was supposed to be about protecting my family. I hadn't done a very good job so far. Maybe vengeance was what was needed.

We were both out of breath and sweaty when we got home.

"Get chased out of town with pitchforks?" My mom chuckled as she dried a glass. My dad snatched it out of her hand and filled it under the tap. He sat at the kitchen table and gulped it down.

"You might want to sit down, too," he said to my mom.

"Is it Roberta?" she asked, her face flooded with worry. "Is Roberta okay?"

"As far as I know, Roberta's fine," he said. She let herself exhale. "Your store, on the other hand—"

"My store?" She sank down onto the chair across from his. "What happened to my store, Al?"

"Molotov cocktail," he said.

"What?" she asked.

He nodded. "It's on fire."

My mom swung her dish towel across the table. It smacked my dad's cheek with a loud *thwap*.

"Is anything salvageable?" she asked.

"I don't know." My dad put his face in his hands. The stovepipe hat tipped forward but didn't fall off. "I don't think so."

My mom got up and paced around the kitchen, hyperventilating. Every once in a while, she passed my dad and smacked his back. He didn't even try to tell her to be nonviolent.

"I'm taking the girls to my father's," my mom finally said. "We're not safe here—what if they bomb our house next?"

"I'm sure that's not going to happen," my dad said.

"How can you be sure?" she yelled. "You told me nothing would happen to the store, either!"

"I couldn't foresee that," my dad said.

"Of course you couldn't," my mom said. "You can't foresee anything but some pie-in-the-sky future that is never going to happen!"

"How dare you say that?" my dad said. "We are making a better future for this town."

"By marching down the street?" my mom said. "By holding signs? By singing songs? How is that ever going to change anything?"

"I'll wait for you to calm down," my dad said. "It's obvious we're not going to be able to have a rational conversation right now."

"My store just burned down!" my mom yelled. "There's nothing rational about that! And all your do-gooding isn't going to bring it back!"

My arms and legs were fizzing—I wanted to hit someone, to kick something, to run and shake myself as hard as I could. I ran upstairs instead. Tabby was reading a picture book.

"We have to pack," I said. "Mommy's taking us to Grandfather's house."

Tabby turned a page. "Why?"

"Her store blew up."

She considered that for a moment.

"I hate the heads at Grandfather's house," she said. The guest room was filled with the heads of animals he had killed—a deer and an elk and a bear. It was hard to sleep with all those dead open eyes.

"We probably won't be there very long," I said, but I had no idea how long we'd really be there. Or when exactly we'd leave.

I looked out the window. Hollister Burgeron was standing on our front walk, just standing there, like he was trying to decide whether to knock. I ran downstairs and out the door. Before Hollister could say anything or run away, I tackled him to the ground. I heard a cracking sound when his head hit the sidewalk—I worried it was his skull breaking. Tears popped into his eyes, so I at least could tell he was still alive.

"Why did you blow up my mom's store?" I yelled in his face.

"I didn't," he said. He started crying, hard.

"I saw you," I said. "I saw you light that match."

"I didn't know my dad was going to do that," he said. "He said it was like a firecracker. It would just make a bang and scare people."

"I hope you go to juvenile hall," I said. It was probably the worst thing you could wish on a kid, other than saying you hoped they'd die. He started crying harder. His chest was heaving, and I was still on top of him, so it made me move up and down, too. It made me feel funny, so I got up.

"He didn't say it was going to blow up," Hollister said, standing and brushing himself off.

"Okay," I said, standing, too.

"Do you think he'll go to jail?" he asked.

"Maybe," I said. "They probably won't let him have a hook there."

"Probably not," Hollister said. He was still sniffling a little.

"Just so you know," I said. "I'm not going to take vengeance on you because I'm nonviolent."

"Thanks," said Hollister.

"But I don't know if I can play with you anymore," I said.

"I know," he said. He leaned toward me like he was

going to tell me a secret. He put a hand on my shoulder. His lips were just an inch from mine. I could smell potato chips on his breath. My heart started to pound a million miles an hour, but then he sighed and turned around and walked away. I could feel his hand on my shoulder and smell his breath for a long time, even after I couldn't see him.

The police showed up at our house. Police, firemen, reporters, the works. Asking questions, taking notes, going over papers. I ran upstairs to get my hat with the press card before they interviewed me—I thought it would look more official. They took some pictures, took some quotes. When I told them about Mr. Burgeron, I didn't say anything about Hollister lighting the match.

I probably shouldn't have been so excited by all the hullabaloo. I couldn't wait to see my picture in the paper. My mom was in shock, though, her face pale, her eyes glazed over. Every once in a while, she started to cry in jagged bursts. My dad tried to comfort her, but she shooed him away like he was a bug.

Roberta disappeared before the commotion died down. Thomas did, too. When it was time for us to leave, my parents checked their rooms and found both of their suitcases gone. Plus Thomas's guitar case.

My mom took me and Tabby to her friend Doris's house, and she and my dad, still in his Honest Abe outfit, went out to search for them. Doris's house smelled like beef brisket and almost all of her furniture was green. She didn't have kids and didn't seem to know what to do with us. She tried to engage us in a game of gin rummy, but Tabby couldn't keep her cards fanned out in her hand and ended up flinging them on the ground. Doris sat us in front of the TV and poured herself a drink. I found a book on her shelf about colon cleansing, which was much more interesting than *Howdy Doody*, so I occupied myself with that.

There was no sign of Roberta and Thomas anywhere. No one had seen them at the train station. No one had seen them at a bus stop. My dad went to the Graue Mill to see if Cindy had hid them in the basement, like the Underground Railroad slaves, but she said she hadn't seen them lately. When my dad showed up in his Lincoln clothes, everyone applauded. He had to put on a sort of show, shaking hands and spewing quotes, even though he was worried about Roberta. He took the hat off before he drove back home so people wouldn't keep pointing at him in the car.

After a night and a day of eating yogurt and celery and Ritz crackers with deviled ham at Doris's house (the only food in her kitchen, pretty much), and watching the store burn down on the news, over and over and over again (the news people particularly liked to show the roof collapsing), my mom getting increasingly hysterical upon each viewing, someone from the Morton Arboretum called to say that Roberta and Thomas were found sleeping in the ash collection. When my mom first told me, her voice so high-pitched it sounded like she had swallowed a whistle, I pictured them sleeping in a giant ashtray or the ruins of Mod Margaret's, but of course they were in the section with all the ash trees on the far east side of the arboretum.

My parents didn't talk in the car on the way to pick them up. Tabby and I played I Spy in the back seat until my mom told us our voices were driving her crazy. Tabby kept yammering until I shot her a "shut up" look. She flinched—I usually didn't give her mean looks like that, but I really didn't want my mom to go crazy. I had kept myself alive, had kept my dad alive. I hadn't counted on Roberta causing the craziness. She was proving herself to be more interesting than she had been as Robert.

Roberta and Thomas both had leaves in their hair and on their clothes. They should have had plenty of time to brush themselves off, but maybe the leaves were their badges of defiance, their proof of living together in the trees. I wondered if they were covered with mosquito bites—I was. There were some holes in the screens of Doris's sleeping porch, so it was kind of like sleeping outside. Roberta was wearing blue jeans. She almost never wore pants, especially blue jeans. She never let her hair get so messy.

Thomas looked very sheepish.

"I'm so sorry, Mr. and Mrs. Edelman," he said when we stepped out of the car. "I didn't mean to cause you any trouble."

"It's all right, Thomas," my dad said. "We know how heady young love can be."

"No, it's not all right!" my mom yelled. I wasn't sure who she wanted to throttle more—my dad or Thomas. "He can't get away with this just because he's your pet project, Al!"

"That's not what he is—," my dad started, but my mom

turned to Thomas, cutting my dad off. "How dare you run away with my daughter? She's just a child!"

"I am not a child!" Roberta yelled. "I'm a nursing student! And I'm the one who said we should run away, not Thomas, so if you're going to get mad at anyone, you should get mad at me!"

"Oh, I'm plenty mad at you, young lady," my mom said. "In fact, I'm so mad at you, I am thinking that maybe nursing school isn't such a good idea anymore."

"Fine!" Roberta said. "I don't want to go, anyway! Thomas and I can find our own place to live!"

"Oh no, you don't," my mom said. "You're going to nursing school whether you like it or not! I'm taking you as far away from this boy as humanly possible."

I felt like my brain was turning inside out. Tabby looked just as confused by my mom's whiplash change of mind. My dad watched helplessly.

"You're sitting in the front with us, young lady," my mom said to Roberta. "And as soon as we get home, your father is taking Thomas back to the city where he belongs."

"Where he belongs?" my dad said. "Thomas belongs everywhere. Don't tell him where he belongs!"

"He belongs away from my daughter," my mom said, pushing Roberta into the front seat.

"I understand, Mrs. Edelman," Thomas said.

"And you can drop the politeness act, Thomas," my mom said. "I know what you really are. You're a predator. A menace."

"He is not," my dad said. "He's a fine young man."

"I bet he couldn't wait to get his hands on some white

skin. That's it, isn't it, Thomas? You came out here to get some white girls, didn't you?"

"Margaret, stop," my dad said.

Roberta started to wail hysterically in the front seat.

"I love your daughter, Mrs. Edelman," Thomas said.

"How can you love her?" my mom said. "You barely know her."

"There's such a thing as love at first sight, Margaret," my dad said.

"And there's such a thing as realizing you've never loved someone at all," my mom said. She slid onto the bench seat next to Roberta and slammed the door shut.

My mom needed to get away from my dad and the reporters and friends who couldn't stop calling to find out more about the store, about how she was doing, about how much loss she had sustained. (All of it, thank you. All of it's gone. Just a couple of links of chain, a couple of hunks of melted Plexiglas survived.) She decided that she would take me and my sisters to live with her dad and stepmother on Lake Shore Drive for a while. So we picked up our things at Doris's house and went home to pack more stuff before we hit the road. My mom wouldn't let Thomas get out of the car. She insisted that my dad drive him home immediately.

Roberta and Thomas both had tears running down their cheeks. Roberta reached one hand back from the front seat and grabbed on to Thomas's. She wouldn't let go until my mom pulled her, sobbing, out of the car.

"I may stay in the city for a while," my dad said, "until things blow over."

"Yeah, I know that's what you want," my mom said. "You just want an excuse to stay with that movement floozy!"

"Margaret—," my dad started. Thomas was quiet, but I could tell he wasn't happy about my mom calling his mom a floozy.

"I knew it!" my mom said. "I knew it all along! You're just as bad as Thomas!"

"It's not what you think," my dad said.

"Oh, what is it then?" my mom asked.

"She understands my desire for justice." My dad looked sheepish.

My mom slammed the car door and stormed off to the house, dragging Roberta with her. Tabby and I stayed in the driveway, not sure what to do.

"Can I go with you?" I asked my dad.

"I'm sorry, Mina," he said before he pulled away. I watched the car turn the corner and wondered how he could just leave like that. How he could just leave me standing there.

We packed and took a cab into the city, to my grandfather's apartment. He sent his maid, Constance, down to pay the fare after the doorman buzzed to say we had arrived. Constance took the service elevator back upstairs with our luggage while we took the fancy one with the elevator operator in a magenta suit. I thought it was strange that rich people didn't even want to push their own gold-rimmed buttons. How lazy can you get?

"Be quiet in the apartment, girls," said my mom. "Behave yourselves. In case I need to remind you, your grandfather and Beatrice are of the belief that children should be seen and not heard."

"That's thtupid," said Tabby. There were a few words her speech therapist hadn't been able to change.

"That's exactly what I'm talking about." My mom touched her lip. "Can the thtupid talk."

Roberta sighed dramatically.

My mom stood outside the apartment door collecting herself, smoothing down her dress, before she used the heavy brass knocker. It was sad that she was so anxious about visiting her own father. If I ever grew up myself, I'd never hesitate before knocking on my dad's door. The maid answered—I wondered how she had had the time to get up there so quickly and put all of the suitcases away. My grandfather and his wife, Beatrice, stood inside, dressed as if they were going to a formal dinner party.

"I knew this day would come," he said to my mom when we walked through the door. Beatrice gave her a confirming raise of the eyebrows. My mom blushed deeply and looked at the floor.

"Thank you for letting us stay, Father," she said.

The apartment was almost as big as our house but wasn't furnished by either Honest ABE's or Mod Margaret's. It looked like it had been furnished by the same people who decorated the White House. Sofa legs carved to look like

bunches of grapes. Gold-scrolled frames around the paint-
ings. Crystal chandeliers. Lots of things we weren't allowed
to touch, including our grandfather and Beatrice, who just
nodded in our direction. Dead animal heads stared glassily
from every wall. No live animals were allowed; we had
dropped Fido off at Phyllis's house on the way.

"Constance will show you to your rooms," Grandfather
said. "Supper will be served at six thirty sharp."

Because we had to be so quiet, Tabby and I tried to do
pantomime with each other instead of talk, but that lasted
about five minutes. Our days there were very long. My mom
spent most of them crying in one room, Roberta crying in
another. Tabby and I spent a lot of time whispering together
inside of closets while the maid cleaned up all the crumbs we
left in the kitchen and my grandfather and his wife took a
nap. One day, Tabby eventually fell asleep, too, on a nest of
my grandfather's winter boots. I wanted to call my dad, but I
didn't know Carla's number. I left Tabby in the closet, with
the door open enough so she could breathe, and went to
look out the window. Lake Michigan was right across the
street, the blue gray water heaving and sighing.

I wandered around the apartment, which was pretty
quiet in itself, except for some soft crying and a vacuum-
cleaner buzz. I looked in all the curio cabinets at the fig-
urines and vases and goblets rimmed with gold. I went into
the bathroom and opened the narrow medicine chest that
hinged on the side of the mirror. It was like an old-lady
pharmacy inside, filled with crimped metal tubes and plastic
pillboxes and face powder. Plus one tiny brown glass bottle,

packed with little white pellets. Nitroglycerin, the label said in bright yellow letters. I knew I didn't have angina, but my heart was aching anyway. What could it hurt to try a few?

I unscrewed the metal cap, tapped three small pellets onto my hand, and set them on my tongue. They tasted like sugar as they dissolved, sugar that been dipped in chlorine and set on fire. I thought they might sear three neat holes right through my taste buds. My whole mouth started to tingle and burn. Heat inched up the back of my neck. My forehead throbbed. The veins and specks of gold in the green-marbled countertop shimmered and twitched. Then the whole room blurred, as if bathed in gelatin. I stumbled into the hall, but my legs didn't work right, so I got down on all fours and crawled to the living room, shadows reeling in front of my face. The gold, textured shag carpet felt like greasy fur under my hands. Tabby, who must have just woken up, ran over and jumped on my back.

"Horsey ride!" she yelled, and I collapsed under her. The carpet turned to moss against my cheek. I could see my step-grandmother, who must have just woken up, too, lean over and look at me quizzically. The last thing I remember is the way her coral lipstick went over the edges of her lips.

I woke up to intense white light. I thought for sure I was dead, in some bright heaven, my Willie destiny fulfilled at last. My throat felt raw. I tried to swallow but couldn't. Maybe angels had a different kind of throat, a different kind of body, one that took a while to get used to. I blinked a few times. My eyelids were easy enough to figure out.

People dressed in white peered down at me. Welcoming angels.

"You're at Presbyterian-St. Luke's," one of them said. I wanted to say I thought you had to go through Saint Peter to get into heaven, but my voice box wasn't working. I must have taken a different entrance. Weird that I ended up at the Presbyterian gate.

"We had to pump your stomach," one of them said, and I thought that was weird, too. Maybe they needed to get all of the human world out of my angel body before I could proceed.

Then my mom leaned into the light, wearing her regular clothes.

"What were you thinking?" she yelled at me, and I wondered if she had died somehow, too. "Nitroglycerin? What in God's name, Mina?"

"I'm going to have to ask you to stand back, ma'am," said one of the angels.

My mom didn't back away. "Do you have a death wish, Mina? Is that it?"

Supposedly all the people you know and love meet you after you die, but I didn't think it would be like this.

"She's going to be fine, ma'am," another angel said. "We'll keep her a day and send her off. She'll be good as new."

I had to wait over a hundred years between Willie and Mina. Time was surely different in heaven. Maybe an angel day was a hundred human years. I wondered who I would be in a day. I felt a sudden twinge—where would Tabby be? How would I find her?

"You have some serious explaining to do, young lady," my mom said, and then she left the pool of light.

"We have a counselor you can speak to," one of the angels said. "As soon as we get this tube out of your throat."

Then I smelled the antiseptic. I shifted my eyes and saw the green walls, the cabinets full of bandages. I felt the tube snake out of my throat, felt my stomach heave and clamp.

I was moved into a more private hospital room with a bed that went up and down and a tray full of Jell-O and beef broth. I didn't feel like eating anything. Talking, either. My stomach and throat both felt like they had been scoured with steel wool. My parents sat in chairs on either side of the bed. I hadn't seen my parents in the same room for a while. Mostly they looked at me, but every now and then I caught them looking at each other.

"What are we going to do with you, Mina?" My mom sighed.

"We're going to love her," my dad said. "And help her."

"There's a therapist," my mom told me, "when you're ready to talk."

I didn't want to talk to a therapist. I just wanted to sleep. Preferably in my own bed. I wanted to forget I had ever taken the nitroglycerin. I wanted to tell them that they should be glad that I was alive, given my history. I wanted to ask where Tabby was. I wondered if Roberta knew what was going on, or if she was off with her friends or Thomas. I wondered if we would have to go back to my grandfather's apartment.

"Thank God you're okay," my mom said. She grabbed one of my hands and my dad grabbed the other, and I could feel the heat of both of them travel all the way to my chest.

After my mom went back to her dad's house, my dad turned on the television. Dr. King was on, giving a press conference. His face was dripping with sweat. My dad looked up at the screen, enraptured.

Dr. King said, "I don't mind saying to Chicago or to anybody, I'm tired of marching. Tired of marching for something that should have been mine at birth. I don't mind saying to you tonight . . . I don't mind saying to you tonight that I'm tired of the tensions surrounding our days. I don't mind saying to you tonight that I'm tired of living every day under the threat of death. I have no martyr complex. I want to live as long as anybody in this building tonight, and sometimes I begin to doubt whether I'm going to make it through. I must confess I'm tired."

I knew just how he felt.

A couple of days after I got out of the hospital, it was time to take Roberta to school. At first my mom was going to fly out with her alone, but then she and my dad decided we should all drive out together. With Roberta leaving, with my parents living in different places, maybe forever, I knew this could be our last chance to be a family.

The drive felt different from other family trips. Usually we had lots of word search puzzles and travel bingo games, and my dad would make up games with license plates, and we would all sing songs together, and stop at Howard Johnson's and buy gifts at roadside gift shops. Sometimes my mom would pack a cooler of sandwiches and drinks and bags of grapes, and it was always fun to eat sandwiches in the car, like some sort of outlaw picnic. This time, though, Roberta sat in the front seat with my parents instead of in the back with us, probably so my parents wouldn't have to look at each other so much. Also so she wouldn't try to get out of the car while it was running, like she did when we first got in the car to leave. There were so many bags and pillows stacked between me and Tabby, I could barely see her. So we stayed pretty quiet in the car, other than occasional sniffling from Roberta and my mom sometimes telling my dad he was going the wrong way and Tabby singing speech therapy songs or saying lists of speech therapy words or narrating what she saw outside—"Cow on the left," "factory shooting smoke," "chicken restaurant with giant chicken on top." I still felt too worn out from the stomach pumping to join in. I spent much of the drive with my head pressed against the window, my eyes sometimes open, sometimes closed.

We drove through Indiana and Ohio and Pennsylvania and Maryland and Virginia, past farms and shopping centers and cities and rivers and towns full of nothing, only stopping to use a bathroom or grab a hamburger. It took a little over twelve hours, all in all. We got there around midnight. Everyone was asleep but my dad.

"We're here," he said, waking us up with his too-loud, too-jaunty voice.

Roberta started crying all over again before her eyes even opened.

"I got us a couple of rooms at the Travelodge," my dad said. "It's too late to check you in to the dorm tonight, Roberta. We'll get you situated in the morning."

"I'll stay with Roberta," my mom said to my dad. "You can bunk with the girls."

My dad looked disappointed, but he didn't say anything—he just handed a key attached to a big blue plastic diamond to my mom. "Come on, girls," he said. I wrapped my arm around Tabby and my dad wrapped his arm around me, and we walked up the pebbly steps to our room on the second floor.

The next morning, my parents were polite to each other, but careful. Even Tabby was being unusually quiet.

"Do you know who Lucy Webb Hayes was?" my dad asked as we drove to Roberta's dorm.

"A famous nurse?" I asked, even though the only famous nurses I had heard about were Florence Nightingale and Clara Barton.

"She was a first lady," my dad said. "And she was a fire-cracker."

My mom rolled her eyes. She didn't seem to have any inkling that she was a first lady herself.

"She was the first first lady to get a college degree," he said. "And she hated slavery. She convinced her husband to become an abolitionist."

"That's good," I said.

"It's more than good," my dad said. "It's wonderful! People loved her."

"More than Mary Todd Lincoln?"

"Much more," he said.

I looked at my mom to see if she looked offended. She did a little, but I don't think it was because we were talking about her. I think it was because we were talking at all.

Roberta's dorm was in a big stone building that looked kind of like a castle. Her room was on the second floor. It didn't look like a castle inside at all—no fancy thrones or gold goblets. The room was small and white with two beds, two dressers, two desks, two lamps, everything neat and plain.

"Do you know anything about your roommate?" my dad asked.

Roberta shook her head. "I don't care," she said. "I don't want to be here." And then she started crying again.

Both my mom and Tabby looked bleary eyed. I touched Tabby's forehead. It felt hot and clammy.

"I think you're sick," I told her.

She shook her head no, but when she stopped shaking it, she looked dizzy. She wavered a little bit before she dropped onto Roberta's bed.

"We're just tired from the drive," my mom said, but then she swallowed hard like something was stuck in her throat.

"Does it hurt?" I asked.

"A little," she said.

My throat was still sore, too, but I could tell it was from the tube in my throat. I pulled my mom into a better patch of light and told her to sit down and open her mouth. Her tonsils were dotted with white spots.

"Just what I thought," I said. "Strep throat."

"I thought Roberta was the nurse in the family," my dad said.

All my time with the medical guide had paid off.

I looked in Tabby's throat, too. She had the same white spots, but even more of them. It made me feel a little dizzy to see anything wrong with her pink insides.

"You need penicillin," I said.

As soon as they realized they were sick, my mom and Tabby started feeling really bad. Headaches, body aches, the sorest throats in the world. My dad took them to Sibley Hospital, where Roberta would be doing her nursing school training, and I stayed with Roberta in her dorm. My dad said he didn't want us to be exposed to more germs if we could help it. Especially me, since I was just in the hospital, myself.

"Keep an eye on her, okay?" my dad whispered to me. "Make sure she doesn't make a run for it." He winked on his way out. My mom followed him like a zombie but didn't let him take her hand. Tabby threw me a rueful, glassy look as she left.

At first Roberta just sat on her bed, teary eyed, staring at the leaves outside the window. Then she said, "I need a phone. Let's look for a phone."

"I'm not supposed to help you escape," I said.

"I'm not escaping, Mina," she said. "I just want to make a call."

I followed her down the long hallway. So many rooms filled with student nurses. Richard Speck would have lost his mind.

I felt a pang. Roberta was going to live here now, on this gray carpet, inside these white walls. She wasn't going to live with us anymore. I could even move into her room at home if I wanted. And even though I barely ever talked to Roberta and when I did she often yelled at me, I could feel some tears starting behind my eyes.

"Do you think you'll be happy here?" I asked her.

"No," she said, and walked even faster. We went down a stairway that smelled like bouillon cubes. A girl wearing a Jackie Kennedy suit was coming up.

"Do you know where a phone is?" Roberta asked. I wondered if she'd be friends with the girl. Probably not if she didn't take the time to introduce herself. Even though the girl looked like someone Roberta would usually hunt down. Someone ceramic.

"Near the office," the girl said. "First floor." She didn't seem very interested in being Roberta's friend, either.

As soon as we found the phone, Roberta told me to scram. I refused—she might run away and then it would be all my fault.

"Just don't listen, then, okay?" she said.

I put my hands over my ears. I know she was talking to Thomas, because she was crying and smiling at the same time, and twirling the cord with her finger like it was her hair, and twisting her toe around on the carpet. Sometimes I cupped my hands over my ears so a few words would come through like "I miss you" and "Come get me" and "Sing to me." Who knew Roberta could be so lovey-dovey?

When she finally hung up, Roberta looked more peaceful than she had for a while.

"Is he going to come get you?" I asked.

"I told you not to listen!"

"I didn't," I lied. "I saw your lips move."

"You should have closed your eyes, too," she said.

I followed her back up the stairs. The soup smell made me hungry.

"And he'll come when he can," she said. "Even if he has to sell his guitar, he'll come."

"Where will you go?" I asked.

"Anywhere," she said.

"It's hard to find a house together if you are white and black," I said. "A lot of places won't even show you a house."

"Then we'll live in a tree," she said.

It was kind of thrilling to hear my sister talk like that, but it scared me, too.

She unlocked the door to her room. Which might not be her room very long if Thomas sold his guitar anytime soon. The girl in the Jackie Kennedy suit was in there. This time she introduced herself.

"I'm Susan," she said. "I guess we're going to be roommates."

Roberta shook her hand. "Roberta Edelman," she said. She took a deep breath, and blinked her eyes a lot, maybe so Susan wouldn't be able to tell she'd been crying.

"Are you Jewish?" Susan asked.

"My dad is," Roberta said.

"Then you're not Jewish," she said. She sounded relieved, which upset me. Why did people always look for ways to not like each other? "It's only passed through the mother."

"We're half Jewish," I said.

"This is my sister Mina," Roberta said. "She's a pest."

"I have one of those, too." Susan smiled.

"Do you have a boyfriend?" Roberta asked.

"Sort of," she said.

"I miss my boyfriend like crazy," Roberta said. "He's amazing."

"There's a lot of cute boys in DC," said Susan. "Med students, primarily. I fully intend to marry a doctor."

"Good for you," said Roberta. "But I'm going to marry a folk singer. A black one. Did I tell you my boyfriend's black?"

Susan looked alarmed at first, but then she seemed more impressed than anything. "I can respect that," she said. Jewish wasn't okay, but black was? At least she wasn't a total jerk.

By the time my dad got back, Roberta and Susan were best friends and I had read most of the book I had brought with me.

"You diagnosed it properly," my dad said. "Streptococci in both throats. Good job, Mina!"

"A lucky guess," said Roberta, and Susan snickered with her.

"Well, don't you seem chipper now?" my dad said, and Roberta glowered at him. Before she could snap, though, Susan stuck out her hand and introduced herself. My dad shook her hand heartily.

"Glad to meet you, Susan," he said. "What are your thoughts on open housing?"

"Daddy!" Roberta yelled. She and Susan gave each other a knowing look.

My dad looked a little sheepish, but then he clapped his hands on his thighs and stood up straight. "I've taken the sickies back to the hotel room. What do you say I take my healthy girls sightseeing? We should get a good look at our nation's capital before we hit the road, don't you think? You can come, too, if you'd like, Susan."

"No thank you, Mr. Edelman," Susan said. "I need to settle in."

"Me too, Daddy," Roberta said. "You should go on ahead." She gave him a long tearful hug and handed him an envelope covered with hearts to bring to Thomas. She hugged me, too. It felt surprisingly good.

"Then I guess it's just you and me, kid," my dad said after we were outside, wiping away tears. "The Dynamic Duo back in the saddle again."

In the car, my dad asked me where I wanted to go. I said anywhere but the White House or Ford's Theatre. He seemed puzzled by this, but I just shrugged. I didn't want to tell him that I wasn't ready to see where we died.

"How about the Lincoln Memorial?" he said.

I was a little worried about going there, too, but it was built long after we were gone. And it was cool that my dad wanted to go there. Maybe the Lincoln part of him was stirring, being so close to our old home.

As we drove toward the memorial, I found my Willie self getting more and more stirred up. Especially when we drove past the White House. It was very white. I wondered if they put a fresh coat of paint every week to keep it so bright and pristine. It probably wasn't as white when we lived there. I pictured me and Tabby as Willie and Tad, running around the East Room, sliding down the banister, shooting cannons off the roof, chopping up the furniture. I pictured myself sitting on my dad's lap, looking up at his beard and his watery eyes as he read to me. I pictured myself dying in my ornate bed while the partygoers ate their oysters and fancy cakes downstairs. I wondered if my dad was having similar thoughts, if he was feeling a pull to that pure white building.

We parked and walked around the mall. I tried to see if I could remember what it was like there before the monuments, before the reflecting pool and paved roads. I closed my eyes and pictured horses and carriages, dirt paths, grass that was a little less green.

"It's beautiful, isn't it?" my dad asked as we approached the Lincoln Memorial. I felt a cramp low in my belly. It looked like the top of Soldier Field, the stadium where we first saw Dr. King speak—it had that same row of thick white columns, like a Greek temple. Dr. King, my dad reminded me, stood in front of the Lincoln Memorial to give his "I Have a Dream" speech just three years before.

"Can you feel it?" my dad asked as we climbed the long steps. "Can you feel his words still filling the air?" He stopped and took a deep breath, his eyes closed.

I tried to feel Dr. King's words, but all I could feel was the pull of the enormous Lincoln statue waiting at the top, glowing in the shadows. I suddenly couldn't wait to be right up next to it. Then my dad started to speak and it stopped me in my tracks.

"Five score years ago, a great American, in whose symbolic shadow we stand today, signed the Emancipation Proclamation."

He made his voice low, like he was trying to sound like Dr. King, but I knew he sounded like he did when he was Lincoln. He was himself talking about himself.

"This momentous decree came as a great beacon light of hope to millions of Negro slaves who had been seared in the flames of withering injustice. It came as a joyous daybreak to end the long night of their captivity."

And you did it, Dad, I wanted to tell him. You sent that great beacon light.

"But one hundred years later, the Negro still is not free." He started to choke up.

You did what you could, Dad, I wanted to tell him. You're still doing what you can. But I could see the tears on his cheeks. He bent forward, his face in his hands. I couldn't stand to see him like that, so I left him standing there and ran the rest of the way up, tears starting to gurgle in my own throat.

My heart was thumping wildly when I stepped inside the memorial. The room was so much bigger than I had imagined. It was like being inside and outside all at once. The air was cool, quiet, even though it was filled with people. I could hear my blood move around inside my head. I felt a little dizzy. The statue of Lincoln was so huge—at least two stories tall—my legs gave way. I plunked down onto the marble floor, felt the coolness of it rise through my jeans. Lincoln loomed and gleamed in front of me like God.

"Are you okay, Mina?" my dad asked when he caught up. He was out of breath, bent over, hands flat on his thighs. He looked so small, so vulnerable, next to his giant Lincoln self.

Lincoln sat on his throne, deep in thought. He was bathed with light but had dark shadows around his eyes; it made him look kind of creepy. His eyes went off to my left a little. I wished he would look right at me. I knew he was marble, but I thought that if he could just see me, he might recognize me, might recognize Willie, and then everything would be all right. His lap looked inviting, but I knew it would be hard and cold if I were to climb up there. His right foot jutted forward, as if he wanted to get up, jump off the platform, stride long-legged down the steps of the memorial. Maybe he'd take a bath in the reflecting pool. Maybe he'd walk right past me without saying a word.

Words were etched in the wall over his head.

IN THIS TEMPLE

AS IN THE HEARTS OF THE PEOPLE

FOR WHOM HE SAVED THE UNION

THE MEMORY OF ABRAHAM LINCOLN

IS ENSHRINED FOREVER

I felt a rush of ownership. Lincoln's memory was enshrined in my heart in a different way, a better way, than it was for the rest of the people. He was my father. Even if he didn't acknowledge me with his eyes.

"Mina." My dad sounded worried. I could smell the sweat of him. He hadn't climbed stairs like that in a long time. I hoped I wasn't putting him in danger by taxing his heart. That would be just too horrible and perfect, if he died inside his own memorial.

I started to sob.

"What is it, sweetheart?" he asked.

How could I begin to tell him?

"I don't want to die!" My voice was gaspy, like an accordion playing air. "I don't want you to die!"

"Oh, honey." My dad crouched down and let me tip against his body, which was warm and soft and a little damp, not at all like marble. "That's not going to happen for a long, long time."

"How do you know?" Before he died as Lincoln, he had a dream in which people were crying and wailing in the White House. When he asked a man in the dream what was wrong, the man said, "The president's been assassinated." And a few days later, he was.

"I don't," he said, and I slumped harder against his chest. "But the odds are good, Mina. We should have a lot of years ahead of us. Assuming you stay away from the nitroglycerin."

I pictured years and years of me worrying about his heart, worrying about my heart, and I felt exhausted all the way through. I thought of Dr. King, sweat dripping down his face, saying "I must confess I'm tired" into a big stand of microphones.

"I want to save you, Daddy," I whispered.

I hadn't done anything to protect him. I hadn't jumped in front of a bullet, hadn't fought off a bad guy, hadn't hidden him in a cellar. I hadn't even prevented a bruise. I had imagined the sheer force of my will would surround him with some sort of impenetrable bubble. What an utter fool I was, an utter failure. Willie would never be so stupid. Never ever ever.

My dad turned to me.

"Mina," he said, taking my face in his hands, "don't you know? You save me every single day."

Tabby, it turned out, had a rash on her chest and back from the penicillin, and my mom had bad diarrhea, and both of them had raging fevers. We were supposed to drive home the next day, but there was no way they could handle being in the car for twelve hours with how they were feeling and how often my mom needed to go to the bathroom. My dad took them back to the doctor, who gave them different antibiotics and suggested sending them home on a plane.

So that's what we did, after another tearful good-bye with Roberta. Phyllis offered to pick them up at the airport and take care of them until we got back. It was very hard to watch Tabby disappear into the plane, barely able to drag herself down the walkway. The thought of her being in the air without me made me nervous, especially since she was sick. What if she had a febrile convulsion? What if she needed someone to hold her tongue? I made a little wish for her Tad soul to keep her safe and sturdy until I could get home and take care of her myself.

It felt normal to be in the car alone with my dad, but it felt different, too, probably because it was my mom's car and smelled like my mom, not him; his car never started working again after it was pulled out of the lagoon.

From Maryland to West Virginia, my dad talked about the ten-point summit agreement that Dr. King had just made with Mayor Daley. The real estate board said it would stop opposing open housing philosophically. The city housing authority said it would scatter public housing around the city rather than keep it all in one place. The country and different agencies said they would help people on public assistance find the best housing possible. Savings and loan places said they'd give loans to anyone, no matter what color.

"Dr. King says it's the 'first step in a thousand-mile journey,'" my dad said. "But at least it's a step."

"That's great, Daddy," I said.

"Of course, not everyone thinks it's great," my dad said. "Some people think Dr. King is selling out. That he agreed too quickly."

"Some people, like Carla?" I asked.

My dad looked wistful for a minute. "Carla's happy for the most part," he said. "Although she's worried about enforcement. She doesn't think the agreement says enough about how all these wonderful things are going to go into effect and what to do if they don't."

"What do you think?" I asked.

"I think," my dad said, "that if they don't do what they say they're going to do, we should go to their offices and bop them in the nose!"

"That's not very nonviolent," I said.

"You're right." My dad sighed. "Then we'll go to their offices and tickle them until they give in." He reached over and tickled my armpit. I squealed and jumped away from him across the seat.

I tried to picture Dr. King going into an office and tickling someone's armpit, but I couldn't do it. He spoke so slowly and deliberately; it didn't seem like it would be easy for him to just run around and laugh. Maybe he spoke that way because he had had speech therapy like Tabby. She was supposed to say her exercises very slow, although she usually rushed through them. I had never heard anyone with a voice like Dr. King's before. I wondered what my voice sounded like when I was Willie. Probably not like Dr. King's. But maybe like my dad's, just a little higher. Maybe if I had grown up, I could have stood in front of great crowds, too. Maybe I still could if I got past twelve in this life.

When we stopped at a diner, my dad ordered cinnamon toast and a side of pickles.

"It's been a while," he said.

When his cinnamon toast came, though, it wasn't like the kind he made at home. They just took regular toast and sprinkled a little bit of sugar and cinnamon on top of the butter. It sat there like dust. It didn't ooze into the bread the way it did when my dad toasted it all together and the cinnamon sugar got all gooey and caramelized. Plus, they brought floppy dill pickle spears, not the gherkins he ate at home. My grilled cheese was different than how my mom made it—the diner used white cheese instead of yellow and put a tomato slice inside—but grilled cheese is good no matter how you make it.

"Well, that sure didn't hit the spot," my dad said, and ordered steak and eggs to take the disappointing taste out of his mouth. It made me happy to hear him say that. It made me think that maybe he was planning to come home to his own toaster. I wondered if Carla had the same kind of Domino cinnamon sugar as we did in our pantry—the yellow plastic shaker shaped like a drum majorette. Did she have gherkins in her refrigerator? Was there a special black brand of pickles, of sugar? Did my dad like them as much as the kind we had at home?

Back in the car, I asked my dad if he thought he was going to move back to Carla and Thomas's apartment when we got home.

"I don't know, Mina," he said. He looked dejected. "I'm not sure she wants me there. I don't think I amuse her so much anymore."

"You amuse me, Daddy," I said, pulling my arm close to my side so he wouldn't try to tickle me again.

"The feeling's mutual, kid." My dad cuffed my arm and smiled, but his eyes still looked a little sad.

I barely stayed awake through Pennsylvania. I fell asleep in Ohio and slept all the way through Indiana and part of Illinois.

I eventually opened my eyes when my dad said, "Wake up. We're here."

"We're home already?" I asked.

"We're in Springfield," he said.

Our pre–White House home. Maybe he knew, after all.

"With all the time you spent on the *Lincoln Log*," he said, "I thought you might want to see what Honest Abe's furniture was really like."

"I know what it was like, Daddy," I said.

"Sure, you read about it in books," my dad said. "But now you can actually see it for yourself. Maybe even sit on it!"

I have already, I wanted to tell him. You have already, too. We all have. Our old souls' bottoms sat on every single chair.

When we walked up to the house at Eighth and Jackson, I expected to feel some sort of spark. Some sort of buzz, like I felt in Washington, that told me I was home. I didn't, though. The house just looked like a house. It was pale brown, not white, as it had looked in the photos. It was much more plain than our house, too—a flat front, no pillars or eaves. When we walked through the house, nothing looked familiar. Nothing felt familiar. Not the furniture I had written about. Not the furniture I had seen in pictures.

"Look at that settee," my dad marveled. "That must be real horsehair upholstery." I tried to remember if it was itchy to sit on, but my skin held no prickle of memory.

In our old playroom, my dad oohed and ahhed over the cane daybed. I looked at the toys propped around the room—a hoop and stick, a little horse on wheels, soldier men—and had no desire to touch them. Not that I was allowed to—I was kept from them by a velvet rope. But I worried that my Willie soul had fallen asleep or worse. If my Willie soul died, would I die soon, too? I jumped around a little to try to stir the Willie-ness inside me.

"Do you have to go to the bathroom, Mina?" asked my dad.

I nodded. I couldn't wait to get out of the house. If I stayed there much longer, I was a goner, for sure.

I let my dad drag me to a tour about the 1908 Springfield race riots. A white woman had wrongly accused a black man of rape; her lie led to thousands of white people burning the homes and businesses of black people, even lynching some. "Abe Lincoln brought them to Springfield," one man shouted, "and we will run them out." The riot lasted two days.

My dad was excited to learn that the NAACP was formed because of this incident, because people like Jane Addams and W. E. B. DuBois signed a letter protesting the injustice of it.

"See?" he told me. "A small group of people can make a difference."

"But riots are still happening now," I said, and his face

darkened. I couldn't help but think of Hollister Burgeron and his dad. Last I heard, Mr. Burgeron was in jail, waiting for his trial. Hollister and his mom had moved away; I saw a big FOR SALE sign on their front lawn when we went home to pack for our road trip. "Good riddance," my dad had said, but it made me sad to see the house so empty, no boys around to stir up the air, no Peter Pan face framed inside the window.

On the way home, my dad took me somewhere even worse—our own tomb. He didn't say where we were going until we drove through the cemetery gates.

The tomb resembled the Washington Monument, except it wasn't as tall, and it had a base with stairs around the bottom holding statues of people fighting in the war and Abe clutching a rolled piece of paper. A big brass head of Abe without a beard sat on a pedestal near the entrance. Most of his face was dull brown, like an old penny, but his nose was like a new penny, shiny and gold. People had been rubbing it for decades for luck. That seemed disrespectful. I hated the thought of so many people rubbing my dad's nose.

Inside the tomb, more statues lined the rotunda hallway leading to the burial chamber—Abe as a young man, Abe on a horse, Abe on two different chairs, Abe standing in front of a chair, gazing at the floor. I could look at the statues, but couldn't stand to look at the tombstone carved with my dad's old name. People had put wreaths of flowers in front of it as if his funeral was being held that very day. The flags of the states where he had lived hung limp behind it. His old body lay beneath it in a steel-reinforced concrete crypt. My old body was interred in the wall behind me. So was my mom's and Tad's and Eddie's. Robert's body was the only one not there—his was in Arlington National Cemetery. The thought of being stuck inside a wall for all eternity made me claustrophobic. I was glad my Willie soul was inside of me, not trapped behind all that marble. But my old body was there. Whatever was left of it.

I forced myself to look at the wall. One marble panel had Mary's name on it. One panel had Willie's and Eddie's, our nicknames carved in smaller letters—EDWARD EDDIE BAKER LINCOLN, 1846–1850; WILLIAM WILLIE WALLACE LINCOLN, 1850–1862. Tad's name was all in big capitals—THOMAS TAD LINCOLN, 1853–1871—on the marble panel he had to himself. I felt jealous until I remembered we were all dead. I thought I might throw up. I wanted to tell my dad we had to leave, but then he said, "Oh, that's sad, isn't it, Mina? Lincoln's sons died so young—three, eleven, eighteen. I can't imagine what that must have been like for him as a father."

Yes, you can, I wanted to tell him—you just blocked it out. "Willie was twelve," I corrected, my lungs tight. That fact was part of my daily knowledge, part of my cellular structure.

"No, he was eleven," he said, handing me an information sheet.

I looked at the paper—born December 21, 1850, died February 20, 1862. I did some calculations in my head and gasped. He was right. I had only paid attention to the years before, not the months. I was eleven years and two months old when I died. This changed everything. I didn't know I was supposed to be careful when I was eleven, I didn't even know I was Willie Lincoln when I was eleven, but somehow I got through the year.

I started laughing and crying all at once, my Willie soul flaring bright. Or maybe it was my Mina soul. A lot of people were crying for the Lincolns, so I probably didn't look too crazy.

"We should hit the road, sweetheart." My dad gently touched my arm. "Let me know when you're ready."

His words caught me off guard. What in the world was I ready for? I didn't know what would be waiting for me when we got home—who I'd be living with if my parents split up, who I'd even be in the next year, myself. My chest started to ache all the way through.

Then I thought about Abe sitting in the train on the way to Washington, DC, when he was just elected president. His life was about to change. So much, he wouldn't know what hit him. But just before he stood up and walked off the train into his new life, he sat there in his velvet chair with Tad and Willie on his lap, and he closed his eyes and breathed in the smell of their hair, and told himself he could do this immense, impossible job.

I suddenly felt very small inside my own skin. Small, but with a good strong heartbeat.

"I will be soon," I told him, eyes closed. But first I pressed my cheek against the cold marble wall and whispered good-bye to my old bones.

THE LINCOLN LOG

A MINA EDELMAN PUBLICATION

Final Edition

EDITOR GETS BAT MITZVAHED

Okay, it wasn't an official bat mitzvah in a temple
and everything, but it was very nice, on Oak Park
Beach in Chicago, Illinois (a.k.a. land of Lincoln),
on the occasion of Wilhelmina Edelman's 13th
birthday. Albert Baruch Edelman (a.k.a. father,
a.k.a. ABE) officiated. No, he is not a rabbi. But
his grandfather was one in Germany, so there might
be some rabbi genes in him somewhere. In attendance
also were Tabby Edelman, younger sister, and
Margaret Edelman, mother. Roberta Edelman, older
sister, was away at Lucy Webb Hayes Nursing School,
but she sent a commemorative Lincoln Memorial coin
to mark the occasion, and her boyfriend, Thomas, sent
a card. Roberta herself was never bat mitzvahed.
Tabby, however, thinks she would like to be.

The ceremony consisted of quotes in Hebrew (which
the bat mitzvah girl mostly didn't understand but
repeated robustly anyway) and quotes from Dr. Martin
Luther King Jr. and Abraham Lincoln. Of the latter,
the honoree particularly liked "In the end, it's not
the years in your life that count, it's the life in
your years," and "Whatever you are, be a good one."
The honoree looks forward to figuring out whatever
it is that she is.

Two receptions were held after the ceremony: chicken and grapes at Margaret Edelman's apartment on the Gold Coast, and then cake and punch at Albert Baruch Edelman's apartment in Hyde Park. Albert got mugged when he first moved in to his place, which nearly gave his middle daughter a heart attack, but now he is settled in and no one gives him any trouble. Especially when his daughters come to stay for the weekend.

While the editor in chief no longer has to write about furniture, she wants to note that Albert Baruch Edelman has set up a furniture-making workshop/store for inner-city youths. He is keeping kids off the streets with saws and nails and inventory books, and so far only one of them has gotten hurt. Plus, he's getting his real estate license. And Margaret Edelman is thinking of opening a Mod Margaret's clothing boutique on a nice quiet street with the insurance money from the fire. She and Albert are also thinking of moving back in together. Maybe, so don't hold me to that. But they did hold hands at the ceremony for a little while.

Tabby and the editor are enjoying their new life as city girls. They are especially fond of Lincoln Park Zoo (which Tabby can now pronounce perfectly). There is one gorilla there, a particularly spiritual-looking gorilla, and when the editor looks right into his eyes, she is sure she knows his deepest, oldest soul.

ACKNOWLEDGMENTS

My Life with the Lincolns only exists because I have so many amazing people in my own life.

Thank you to Anika Streitfeld and Arielle Eckstut, for encouraging me to write this book and sending it on the path toward its rightful home. Thank you to Ellen Geiger, for bringing the story to Holt, and finding the perfect editor, Kate Farrell, to bring it to life. I'm so grateful for you both and all of your enthusiasm. Thank you, too, to Sarah Dotts-Barley, who has been so wonderful at Holt, as well.

Thank you to the Virginia Center for the Creative Arts, for giving me time and space to work on the novel (and to Kelly Grey Carlisle, for daring me to put a rhinoceros in the story while we were both fellows there. I'll be looking for a rhinoceros in your book now!)

Thanks to Elizabeth Brandeis and Laraine Herring, for reading early drafts and giving such meaningful, useful feedback.

Thank you to Miles Harvey, Matt Harvey, and Scott Whitlock for sharing first-hand accounts of growing up in

Downers Grove in 1966, and to Tinker Harvey and Ralph Stein, for sharing your stories about working for open housing there.

Thank you to the women of CODEPINK: Women for Peace and the Women Creating Peace Collective, for showing me what a difference people can make when they join their voices together.

Thank you to everyone—friends, family, students, colleagues—who has nourished my life with support and love.

Special thanks to my dad, Buzz Brandeis (who I still secretly think used to be Abraham Lincoln), and my mom, Arlene Brandeis—I am so grateful for all of your encouragement. Thanks to Matt McGunigle, for his early faith in me. Endless thanks to my daughter, Hannah Brandeis-McGunigle, for inspiring me to write a "family-friendly" story (and for finding the manuscript of this book on my computer when I thought it had been lost forever), and to my oldest son, Arin Brandeis-McGunigle, for all of his encouragement, in general. Sweet thanks to my new son, Asher Brandeis, for his surprise entrance into our lives, and to my husband, Michael Brandeis, for his beautiful, loving heart.

And a deep, deep thank you to Abraham Lincoln, Martin Luther King Jr., and everyone else who has worked so hard for equality and justice. May we continue to move your important work forward!